MINT DEATH

JILL QUINT, MD FORENSIC PATHOLOGIST
BOOK FOURTEEN

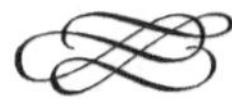

ALEC PECHE

ACKNOWLEDGMENTS

I'd like to thank Grace for giving me ideas for this story.

I'd like to thank Ellen Falk for her editing. My manuscript was a nightmare before she fixed it. While my imagination is endless, my knowledge of grammar sadly is not.

Alec
     March 2023

MINT DEATH

Ed Thomas was standing in front of the cutter. He was an employee of the United States Treasury's Bureau of Printing and Engraving in Washington D.C. The cutter was taking sheets of twenty-dollar bills and cutting them into single notes. The machine did all the work; he was there just to stop it if it got jammed or wasn't otherwise properly working. He'd been doing this exact job for fifteen years.

He'd awoken with a little feeling of being off, but brushed it off and went to work. Now he was feeling dizzy and that sensation proceeded to get worse. So he hit the stop button on the machine as he needed to sit down, and he couldn't sit down without turning the machine off first. He hit the off button and before he knew it, collapsed to the floor. His teammates looked over when they saw the machine stop. They wore ear plugs on the job to protect their hearing, so the hum of machinery was a little less noisy once the cutter came to a halt, though it took them a while to notice. The first person who looked over didn't see Ed anywhere and assumed he had stopped the machine for an emergency bathroom break as that occasionally happened. When the machine hadn't restarted ten minutes later, someone went looking for Ed.

"Oh my God, Ed, did you fall?" Aaron said, shaking his arm. When there was no response he shouted, "Someone call 911." Others rushed to join Aaron, while the call was made to emergency services. There was a complex protocol to let emergency responders inside the building. With millions of dollars of cash lying around, an armed security escort was required. Every employee at every stage of the money-printing process was required to stand at their station and make sure that no one left with newly printed bills. It slowed the responders arriving at Ed's side by perhaps a minute, but it didn't matter. Ed had died five minutes ago.

CHAPTER 1

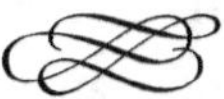

Jill Quint, MD, forensic pathologist and vintner, was in her kitchen drinking coffee and reading email. Her new husband, Nathan Conroy, would be asleep for a few more hours as he wasn't the morning person that she was. It was raining outside, which was an event to always be celebrated in California. The ever-present drought had been the weather news for at least half of her forty-five years. She would accomplish no work on her vineyard until the afternoon, when the rain was projected to stop. By then Nathan would be at work and she could daydream about her tasting room, which she was going to start building as soon as the permits were approved by the county.

Her phone rang, and the caller ID read "Washington DC." There was a national election in another month and she and everybody else was getting hit with spam calls about candidates. She wondered if this was one of those? She sighed and connected the call.

"Hello."

"Hello? I would like to speak to Dr. Jill Quint."

Oh gosh, this was going to be a spam call.

"Yes, this is Dr. Quint," Jill said in a clipped voice. She hoped it portrayed her annoyance with the caller.

"My name is Melanie Thomas. My father died on the job yesterday. The police seem to think he had a heart attack. They won't listen to me when I tell them that my dad was getting threats."

Jill felt bad. She had been rude in the way she answered the phone and was abrupt with the potential client. She sat up straight, grabbed her pen and paper that were next to her and started to take notes and ask questions.

"Ms. Thomas, I'm so sorry for your loss. How old was your father? And did he have a heart condition?"

"He was fifty-two and he had no history of heart disease. My grandfather is still alive and well."

"Would you know if the local coroner has completed the autopsy on your father?"

"I don't know. The police are not telling me much."

"You said your father was getting threats. What kind of threats? Were they over the telephone? Did he receive threatening emails? Did someone knock on his door and threaten him?"

"He was getting letters in the mail."

"Do you have copies of the letters? What did the sender want him to do? Where did he die?"

"My father was found dead at work. He operates the cutting machine at the US Bureau of Printing and Engraving. As sheets of new dollar bills come through his machine, it cuts them into individual bills. His co-workers said that they noticed the lack of sound which meant the machine was turned off. They thought dad needed an emergency bathroom break as that would be the only reason to turn the machine off unscheduled. When he didn't return after ten minutes, they went looking for him and found him dead on the floor. They called emergency services, but it was too late. Dad was already dead."

"I'm so sorry for your loss. It sounds like it is early into the investigation of his passing. Are you sure the police are not inter-ested in his death?"

"Yes. Dad listed me as his next of kin. I heard about his death when the police knocked on my door. They said with surety that dad had had a heart attack and died on the job. When I asked them about the threatening letters he had mentioned receiving, they didn't seem interested. I mean, they didn't ask me for copies or even where the letters were located. Wouldn't you assume that meant that the police were not interested? They saw no reason to view his death as suspicious."

Jill thought that sure sounded like a lack of interest. But she was never one to bash a police department until she formed her own personal opinion.

"That does seem odd. Do you have the letters that he mentioned? If you do, you should handle them wearing gloves and put them in a safe spot."

"I'll go over to his house and look for them now. The reason I called is I found you via a Google search. I read a few stories about you online and you seem to leave no stone unturned. I'd like to hire you to make sure my dad's death is fully investigated. What should I do next?"

Jill had many questions, including could this young woman afford her rates as an investigator. She said she was next of kin, but did she have power of attorney to give Jill access to her father's remains, as well as his possessions?

"The next step is typically that I discuss my investigation rates, and then, if that is acceptable to you, I'll send you a contract to sign which is your way of hiring me. Additionally, I require a retaining fee up front. I'll also have you sign some forms that are for the medical release of information. If by the time I get there, the county medical examiner has not finished his forensic exam, I'll try to join that examination. If they are finished, then I'll contact the funeral home that you want to use and see if I can get their permission to perform an autopsy on their premises. What do you think about that?"

That was Jill's way of trying to ask respectfully about whether the victim's daughter could afford her services. It sounded like a case that would interest her, and if it was local, she might've done it for free. However, if she had to fly across the country from California to Washington DC, book a hotel, and find somewhere in the District to process her test results, then the costs would start adding up quickly.

The young woman agreed to Jill's terms and gave her contact information so she could sign the contract.

"I look forward to receiving your contract and I'll get it back to you."

"It would be cheaper if you hired someone local to DC. Are you sure you want to hire me?"

"Yes. Besides his autopsy, there's the greater mystery of the threats my father was sent. I need an investigator to look into those threats, and you seem to be able to hit all the checkboxes at once."

They wrapped up their conversation, and Jill sent her standard contract to Melanie Thomas. She did a quick search on the woman before she sent the contract out. It seemed like a weird case, and Jill didn't want to be caught up in anyone's shenanigans. She waited for the contract to be sent back to her along with the money wire to cover her upfront fee. Well, maybe the woman was independently wealthy, or had a famous patent to her name. It was kind of weird that her father worked at a currency machine for the US Treasury, and the daughter was wealthy enough to hire a California consultant to investigate her father's case. She also found it weird that the woman didn't sound like she was grieving over the phone. Of course, everyone grieved in their own manner.

Her search on Melanie revealed her to be an entrepreneur. She was successful with non-fungible tokens. OMG, Jill was going to have to research those to understand what it was. Regardless, it was Melanie's source of funding for Jill's investigation.

By the time Nathan was awake, Jill had her travel plans, and her retainer fee deposited into her bank account. While Nathan often joined her on cases, she knew he had a lot of appointments scheduled over the next few days. He was a prominent wine label artist, was a professor of creative marketing at the University, and also was mentoring students in wine industry marketing. She took a moment to write an email to her friends—Marie, Angela, and Jo—about the new case. She also checked in with Madison Lewis.

Madison was likely about the same age as the victim's daughter, Melanie. Jill met Madison during her last case in Asheville, North Carolina. Jill worked out a contract to train Madison in private investigator work. She would have to get to DC on her own dime—she would likely drive—but this case had all the markings of an excellent learning opportunity. Madison planned to pick Jill up from the airport that evening, and the two of them would head to their hotel to meet their client first thing in the morning. Madison's family had connections in the hotel world, so they had a great hotel at a good rate.

Jill kissed Nathan goodbye and headed to the airport for the long flight to the East Coast. She kept her autopsy kit packed and ready to go in the trunk of her car. She took it out and sorted a few things as she wouldn't be collecting evidence and bringing it back to her lab in California. She already notified a DC-area laboratory of her needs, and had an arrangement for processing any specimens she might collect during Ed Thomas's autopsy. She settled in for the five hour flight and wondered what she would find by the time she got there. Before she had left home, she printed some material on how paper money was made in the United States. She wanted to understand what chemicals were used in the process to see if any of them had the potential to kill someone. She doubted that, as Melanie said her father had worked for a while at the US Bureau of Printing and Engraving, so it couldn't be a sudden allergic reaction.

She felt well-versed in the process of making money by the time her plane touched down at Dulles airport. Madison was waiting in a cell phone lot and soon arrived to pick up Jill and her luggage at the curb.

"How's it going? Your flight was on time and that's always good," Madison said.

"It was a nice flight, and more importantly, my luggage arrived with me. I would've been delayed if I didn't have the autopsy kit. I thought I would include you in the autopsy as my assistant. Are you OK with that? Have you seen a dead body? I'll lose a little cooperation from people here if my assistant passes out."

"I've never seen a dead body, so I can't predict my reaction. A couple of years ago. I volunteered at our local hospital because I wanted community participation points for high school. Nothing I saw at the hospital made me sick, but I didn't see any dead bodies."

"I don't know yet if I will join the medical examiner for the autopsy, or if I'll be doing a second autopsy on our victim at a funeral home. Lately, I have enough of a reputation as a forensic pathologist that a local medical examiner usually allows me to watch, and sometimes even assist during an autopsy. Depending on the environment here, you may or may not be able to observe. If you feel sick at any time, please leave the room. I wouldn't want you injuring yourself by fainting on the tile floor."

"Got it. When are we meeting the client?"

"Tomorrow. I thought about scheduling it for tonight, but that can be tricky depending on flight schedules. I'd rather wait to arrive, then confirm my meeting time with a client. I informed her that you would be joining me as an intern, and that she wouldn't be paying your salary."

"I have all of your information that you sent me. I looked up information about the US Bureau of Printing and Engraving.

Unlike most murder scenes, I don't see us being allowed in to examine where Mr. Thomas worked. Would you agree?"

"I would think they have an interesting protocol for handling emergencies in the building. It's a very high security situation and you don't want first responders to grab freshly printed money as they respond to emergencies. It has to be tempting to walk by a stack of hundred-dollar bills and want to reach out and grab them and stuff them in a pocket."

"Yes, that is an interesting aspect of this case. It wouldn't have made a difference in whether Mr. Thomas lived or died, from what I read in the files that his daughter sent to me. I can't imagine what it's like if you're Security, and you have to escort unexpected visitors past millions of dollars."

"Who do you think did it?" Madison asked.

"First we have to prove there was an 'it.' At this point, we don't know that we have a murder on our hands, right?"

"We know we have a dead body, but we don't know how it got dead."

"I like that summation. That was very good, Madison."

"Thanks!"

"Let's grab some dinner."

It was later than she liked to eat, but then again, it wasn't late if she considered California time. They consulted with the hotel and found a place close by with great food.

"Have you heard from the medical examiner?" Madison asked.

"I have not heard just yet, and given the time of night, I don't think I will hear from them before tomorrow. Often when I talk about observing an autopsy, the local medical examiner feels the need to run that by the higher ups."

"Why? You have the family's permission."

"I do have it, but that's only the first piece of it. The autopsy takes place on the physical grounds for the medical examiner, and they have the right to say yay or nay to my being there. Sometimes they don't want to do an autopsy in front of me for fear that

I will find something they don't. Other times the office thinks they might learn something from me and so they welcome me into the autopsy. I don't get upset if they deny me permission as they have the legal right to do that. It just means that I'll have to make arrangements to do a second autopsy at a funeral home and send any specimens that need analyzing out to a local lab or fly them back to California to my lab. If I'm an hour away by plane, then going home makes sense. But commuting five hours from the East Coast and then another hour from the airport to my home just so I can process specimens in my home lab doesn't make sense. Do you know what we're going to do once we are done with the autopsy?"

"Normally, I would think the next thing a private investigator would do is visit the scene of the crime. However, the scene here is the Bureau of Printing and Engraving, and we're not going to be let in, unless the police escort us," Madison said.

"In normal times, you're correct, and we would visit the scene of the crime next. However, if we can jointly do the autopsy with the local medical examiner, then we might have evidence from that autopsy that makes the death look like it's suspicious. In that scenario, the medical examiner would call the police and we would try to stay connected as long as we could. Our loyalty is to our client and to the truth."

"I like that. Our loyalty is to the truth. Someday when I set up my own detective agency, I'll make that my tagline. Hopefully that will keep the idiots who are guilty away from hiring me."

"That's not always the case. I had a case in Dallas. The husband hired me and he was the murderer. She discovered his drug-smuggling secrets and so he poisoned her with arsenic laden muffins. She fell over dead as she was giving a speech to her medical colleagues. It was really quite shocking."

"Seriously? If I wanted to cover up a crime, you would be the last person I would hire. Stupid man. He should've hired Bob's

Bail Bonds and Private Detection. *He* certainly wouldn't turn his attention toward the man paying his bills."

"You'll find in time that you get all kinds of crazy clients in this business. My first word of advice is to develop a contract to be used between you and the client that meets the laws of North Carolina first because that's where you're headquartered, and eventually as many states as possible.

"So the laws vary from state to state? Does that mean I have to get a PI license in every state I work?"

"Not necessarily, there's a lot of reciprocity between states and there are a few states that don't require licenses at all. You also want to be clear in your contract that you require a stipend to start a case. My stipend varies depending on where the case is located. I was called to Sicily and I started with a large retainer due to the travel and the client wanted the entire team there. If the case is local, then I might require a fairly small amount to cover a day's work, depending on the case. Don't tell the clients this, but sometimes I have a need to get at the truth and so I provide my services for free."

"I can see myself doing the same as you do in regard to the retainer. My services will always be cheaper than yours, though, because I'm not a forensic pathologist and I can't do expensive testing that a client may need. Maybe I need to subcontract you to process my work, or do an autopsy on one of my cases." Madison said.

"You'll get cases that make sense to bring me in for a portion of the investigation after you get your PI license. However, you may find local resources that are cheaper than flying me in from California. However, that's pretty far in the future. I don't know what the laws are in North Carolina, but in California you need to work for a licensed PI for two years before you can apply for your own license. Have you researched it?"

"I have. I need to have three years of experience conducting investigations. Part of that can be criminal justice classes at college. I took a couple of classes and so I need the state board to evaluate how much in-person training I need. This case will really help me get off to a good start and collect those hours. I also need to ask how I document my experience working for you."

"I don't have a license in North Carolina, so will that be a problem with your training?" Jill asked.

"No. I'm not required to get the training in my home state. They accept military experience and no one is stationed in their home state for that. I just have to have it, so it doesn't matter that you're not licensed in North Carolina.

Jill paused to look at her email, but there still was nothing from the medical examiner. If she didn't have an answer by ten the next morning, she would get on the phone and start harassing people and find out where Mr. Thomas's remains were located.

CHAPTER 2

*J*ill had had a nice conversation with Nathan before she went to sleep the previous night. They caught up on each other's lives, and she saw in the background Trixie and Arthur positioned in their usual standoff. Nathan was a night person, so she wouldn't be talking to him before noon on the East Coast.

Jill met Madison for a run around the National Mall. Jill was shorter and older, but she was in shape and so she could keep pace with Madison.

While they were out running, Jill received word that she was not going to be allowed into the medical examiner's office to observe the autopsy. She could examine the man's remains at the funeral home later that day.

"Our client gave me the name of the funeral home she's going to use. I'll contact them now about performing an autopsy. They will be distressed by it, because it's likely never a request they have had before, but I've yet to have anyone turn me down. So you absolutely can watch and I'll explain what I'm doing."

"This will be a really interesting day. Just observing you interacting with the client and seeing my first autopsy and dead body."

"Yeah, by the end of the day, you might decide that this profession isn't for you. It shouldn't contain danger to yourself like I've run into in other cases, though. There's always complications—sometimes law enforcement doesn't want to cooperate, sometimes you have untrustworthy clients, and sometimes you can't get cooperation from the medical examiner's office. You just have to roll with it and see what you have. It also helps if you have team members like I do whom I can discuss a case with. Even after your training, feel free to call me for advice; you'll eventually want to hire people to help you. As my friend Jo says, so many crimes are related to money, so finding someone to look at that aspect for you is critical to solving cases. My friend is not a forensic accountant, which has worked just fine for me. I think if I were the police or the district attorney, I would need to have a certified forensic accountant to prosecute a case. But I'm not doing that and so just a really smart financial person will help you," Jill said.

"Remind me again of what the other people on your team do?"

"In her day job, Marie evaluates people for employment. Part of that evaluation is checking out everything a candidate posts on social media. I call her my social media maven. It's just another way to unearth information about a group of people who may be involved in your investigation.

"Angela is a photographer in her day job, and so she's really good at taking pictures at exactly the right time so we can see who is around us. She's also a great interviewer. She could ply secrets out of a Soviet spy."

"Is that it? I thought you had other people on your team."

"I have other people, but I don't employ them per se. Henrik is an IT genius. He's given me some software for facial recognition that far exceeds anything you can buy on the open market. He's also been able to unlock some phones for me. You also met Melissa, a former forensic psychologist when she's not running her vineyard. She can help me work through motivation. It always helps to understand motivation as that often connects the killer. I didn't always have Henrik and Melissa, but I gathered them as my career progressed, and so will you."

"When you started out, it was just you, and you only did autopsies to provide a second opinion on the cause of death, right?"

"Yes. Then I brought my friends on board and after about three years, I got my PI license as that seemed to satisfy some law enforcement."

"And all this time you've also been planting grapes and making wine? Why?"

"So, you know I used to work as a forensic pathologist in the government. However, the paperwork and the court testimony were a waste of my talent. When I was in medical school, in the back of my head, I always knew I wanted to use my botany degree to run a vineyard. When I got fed up with the paperwork, I bought a winery and went to work on my second career. Then someone in my former office called me in for a case and that was the start of my reputation. I also guess that I was going to do this all along, because when I built my lab to study pesticides and additives for my wine crop, I also bought equipment that is used in autopsies for analysis."

"That's a pretty cool second career. Live grapes and dead bodies."

Just before Madison uttered that last sentence, they had reached the end of the run and the doorway of their hotel. A man at the door did a double take at Madison's last statement. The two women smiled at each other and went upstairs to change. They were going to meet their client in an hour.

Melanie Thomas was roughly the same age as Madison. She seemed impressed that Jill was training Madison and was pleased that she was potentially finding a new career with Jill's help.

"Tell me about your father, Melanie. How long did he work for the Bureau of Printing and Engraving? Did he like his job and his co-workers? Tell me anything you can think of about his job. Then we'll move on to your family," Jill said.

"My mother had me when she was young and she told my dad about me as they had lost contact with each other. It wasn't anything my father did; it was just the circumstances. Before I went to college, I looked up my father and we grew closer to one another, and we would have adult dinners generally once a week. I didn't know he had named me as next of kin, but I guess I'm not surprised, as I am his only daughter."

"Only daughter or only child, or both?" Jill asked.

"Both. I am his only offspring. He has brothers and sisters, but none in this immediate area."

"When did he tell you about the threats that he received?"

Melanie was quiet for a bit, obviously thinking.

"I guess about two months ago. I don't know how long the threats had been happening, as now that I think about my father's conversation, he never said that the letter he was speaking about was the first letter he received. Sad to say, I don't know how long the threats were going on."

"Were you able to collect any of the letters after we talked?"

This question was apparently the breaking point for Melanie. Her eyes filled with tears and ran down her face.

"I did like you suggested and went over to his house, but when I got there, it was clear that someone was there before me as stuff was tossed all over the place."

"I'm so sorry, Melanie. Did you call the police?"

"I did, and the police took some time to arrive. As no one was harmed and far bigger crimes were occurring, they weren't in a hurry to respond. I don't think there will be any follow-up."

"Did you notice if the police took photographs or fingerprints?"

"They were advising me to have the locks changed, then they got a call that was more important or a bigger problem than mine, and they left before they could collect any evidence."

"I'd like to go over there this morning if it's okay with you. I'll be doing the autopsy on your father as soon as the medical examiner's office releases him to the funeral home. Why don't you just give me the key and I'll text you if I have any questions," Jill suggested.

"It's okay. I'll go with you. I just had a minor breakdown over this entire situation. I sort of get that the police have serious crimes to deal with and my father's death doesn't appear to be something for them to follow up on. Furthermore, the robbery of his apartment likely seems minor in light of the felonies that occur in the District every day."

"Thank you, Melanie. Is there parking available at your father's apartment building?"

"No, but there's usually street parking."

Okay, why don't we go take a look at his apartment. We'll follow your car more or less until we start hunting for a parking space. I have more questions for you and will continue asking you while we examine your father's residence. How does that sound?"

"That sounds great. I'll write down the address in case we get separated." She did that and passed the paper to Jill. She added, "I have to clear the apartment eventually and having you asking questions will make it go better for me."

They followed the directions that Melanie gave them to a congested residential area of the District. They had to search for parking for about five minutes before they found a spot. They walked back to Mr. Thomas's building and waited for Melanie to find her own parking spot and meet them at the building.

They were surprised by the condition of Mr. Thomas's home. It had been tossed as Melanie mentioned. She wasn't kidding that she had not cleaned anything up. Paperwork and contents were strewn across the apartment.

"Is this the same condition it was in when the police were here yesterday?" Jill asked.

"It's kind of hard to tell as it's such a mess. I don't think anything is worse than it was yesterday."

"What kind of housekeeper was your father?"

"He served in the military when he was younger, and he never let go of neatness. He would have a heart attack if he saw the condition of this apartment. He never left stuff lying around and at most there was a coffee cup in the sink."

"What did the police say when they saw the condition of the apartment?"

"They saw it as a simple robbery unrelated to his death. I don't know what they see in their everyday lives as police officers, but I can't imagine that most burglars go to this much trouble to find stuff. It would've taken hours to do this and there's risk from being found inside someone's home. Wouldn't you agree?"

"Yeah. I've seen some searches in my short life as a private investigator, and this looks like more than a burglary. Let's start searching ourselves and see if we can find anything of concern. Maybe we can help you straighten it out somehow, too. Do you have any ideas?"

"Why don't we put things back where they obviously belong, and put books and paper in a stack to go through slowly. Would that help you, Miss Thomas?" Madison spoke for the first time.

"I can't think of a better idea."

"Before we start, everyone should have some gloves in case we come across something suspicious. Here is a pair for each of you to wear. Melanie, did your father mention what the threatening letters looked like? Were they typed or handwritten? On colored paper? Did they come in an envelope? Were they emails?"

"He didn't say. Let me think a little bit about the conversation and maybe I'll think of some hint that would answer your question."

The three women got to work, each in a different room of the apartment. In short order, things were looking better. Jill had sent Melanie into her father's bedroom as that was likely where his most personal possessions were located. She would occasionally stop the organizing she was doing and go ask Melanie a question.

"Tell me a little more about your family. Both of your parents, any siblings, any siblings to your father."

"My parents weren't married when my mom got pregnant. By the time she knew she was pregnant, my father had already enlisted in the military and was out of contact. There was no cell phone or email, and so we pretty much forgot about him. She later remarried and I have two half siblings. My stepfather is a nice guy. However, I got curious in my teenage years about my real father, and so with the help of the Internet, I began searching for him. Mom lived in Baltimore, and he lived in the District. They were separated by perhaps ten miles, but they had never run into each other after their experience with young love. I first met my father shortly after I graduated from high school."

"Did your father remarry? You don't have any half-siblings on that side of the family, right?" Jill asked.

"Surprisingly no. I don't think he forgave himself for losing my mom. When I had them meet each other, I could tell my mom had moved on 100 percent with my stepfather. My father was immediately back at age eighteen. He kept it to himself, and my parents don't see—didn't see—each other. It's kind of weird to talk about it in the past tense."

"So you've had the opportunity to get to know your father in these last six or seven years. He's worked at the US treasury that entire time, right?"

"Yes, to me his job sounded kind of boring, but he got a thrill out of watching millions of dollars being made every day. I guess whatever floats your boat. I was happy that he was happy with his job. When he left the military, he told me he didn't know what he wanted to do with himself. The government had a push to hire veterans and so he looked into the Bureau of Printing and Engraving. He did a variety of jobs for them before he became master of the cutting machine. He said it was a very important job. Everyone else's work that came before his job depended on his machine cutting the bills correctly."

"Did he like his co-workers?"

"He did. He felt like they were a team, all making something important and useful to the average American. He said he felt as patriotic about making money as he did about serving in the military."

While they were chatting, they had begun setting some order to the apartment. Jill took a video of the apartment before they started as evidence in case they needed it later in the case. Now they had somewhere to sit in the living room and piles of food and baking supplies had either been tossed or put back in their place. You don't have this kind of damage in an apartment without someone doing a deep search for something. Jill bet that it was the letters that Mr. Thomas had received before his death.

While she was cleaning up, she was thinking about what could have happened inside the Bureau of Printing and Engraving that could cause a man's death. No one else was sick or killed at his jobsite. That eliminated a lot of weapons. Further, it pointed to a fellow employee as the murderer, as there was such high security that no one else could have gotten inside. Someone didn't like Mr. Thomas. The question was, who?

"I think I found something," Madison's voice rang out.

Jill and Melanie hurried to the kitchen. Madison was standing next to a package of frozen food that had defrosted once the intruders had left it on the floor. They could see something in a baggie inside the folds of a large package of chicken breasts. It was one of those packages that had two to three skinless chicken breasts inside a package. There were three individually sealed packages folded together and taped for six packages in total. They could see how the baggie would've been missed when the package was frozen. Fortunately, before Madison had thrown the entire package of chicken out, she had searched it and found the baggie.

"Let me put on a fresh pair of gloves to handle what's inside that baggie. I'm sure all of our original gloves have gunk on them and especially your gloves, Madison, as you've been handling spoiled food."

Madison removed her latex gloves, tossing them into the garbage, and put on a new pair as Jill held the package of chicken open. Madison removed the baggie and looked around for a clean place to unfold the papers. She saw the coffee table in the living room and headed there.

The three of them read the first page of one of the letters. This confirmed that Mr. Thomas was receiving threats.

"I think we should give the police one more chance to do the right thing with your father's death. Let me call them and see what I can stir up," Jill said. "But before we do that, I'd like you to make a phone call to the medical examiner's office and see if they have any findings from the autopsy, as that would add weight to our discussion with the police.

CHAPTER 3

*I*t took some time for the verification of next of kin for the medical examiner's office to give Melanie any information. His cause of death was undetermined. The call was on a speaker phone so Jill and Madison could listen. Jill passed a note to Melanie to ask the office:

"Did you confirm he had a heart attack?"

"We confirmed he didn't have a heart or brain attack."

Jill passed her one final question: "Will my father's body be released to the mortuary today?"

"Yes. It says here that he was already picked up by the mortuary."

"Thank you."

Jill nodded as Melanie pressed the disconnect button. She was scrolling on her phone as the call came to an end.

"Let's call the non-emergency number for the District police department and see if we can make an appointment with a detective. They should want to get on the case," Jill said as she held out her phone for Melanie to dial the number.

Melanie did as instructed and an appointment was set up for later that day with a detective at the police headquarters. It didn't sound like they were going to be enthusiastic about the case, but Jill always liked to bring the official people in on any case, as she never knew when she was going to need them.

Meanwhile, they called the mortuary to see if Jill could use their premises later that day to perform an autopsy.

"We haven't received a call to pick up the body yet, so I can't confirm the time for you."

"Are you sure? We just spoke with the medical examiner and they said the mortuary picked up my father."

"I'm sure. Maybe they called the wrong mortuary, though it's strange as they would need your permission to pick up your father if you are the next of kin. Did another family member make different arrangements?"

"No. He wasn't married and I'm his only child. I don't think one of his siblings would have made arrangements, but I'll check," and Melanie ended the call with the mortuary.

"That's strange. When I got word that Dad died, I called one of his brothers, and he said just let him know what the funeral arrangements were. No one said they were going to do the funeral arrangements themselves. I don't understand."

"Can you give your uncle a call and see if anyone made arrangements?" Jill asked.

"Sure I'll do that right now."

It was apparent about ten minutes later that no one else had made funeral arrangements. "I think we'd better go down to the medical examiner's office and ask to see the paperwork," Jill said.

"Do you want to call the police before or after the ME's office?" Madison asked.

"Let's wait. We may have an entirely different crime to talk to the detective about if your father's remains are missing. As a consulting forensic pathologist and private investigator, I have completed perhaps one hundred cases in my second career and this is the first time I've seen a potentially missing body on my watch."

They gathered up their belongings with Jill taking the threatening letters and placing them in her purse after photographing the contents. This time they set off together in Melanie's car as they would be going from the medical examiner's office to the police and likely back to the apartment all on this day.

A short time later they pulled up in front of the DC medical examiner's office. It was a four or five-story building, boring in its glass and concrete exterior. There was a reception area just inside the door and Melanie indicated what the problem was—her father's body was missing and she wanted to see the paperwork of the people that had picked them up that morning.

Melanie's question sent off a flurry of activity. The receptionist typed a message on her keyboard and then made a call for someone inside.

They took a seat while they waited for someone to come out and speak to them. An employee did just that after checking Melanie's ID and the paperwork, indicating that she was her father's next of kin. The employee went back inside and was gone for a full fifteen minutes. Jill wondered how hard could it be to find the paperwork of something that happened that morning?

The employee came out with someone in tow, and introductions were performed.

"Miss Thomas, my name is Susan Rock Taylor and I'm a clerk with the medical examiner's office. I have copies for you of the mortuary that your father's remains were signed out to this morning. Can you tell me if you recognize the name of the mortuary or the people?"

Melanie looked at the paperwork, including the name of the mortuary and its address. She was fairly sure that the address represented a vacant lot in Baltimore. She knew that because it was close to where she had grown up and she knew that neighborhood pretty well. It was an interesting choice of an address.

Melanie looked at the clerk and said, "I think we have a problem here. That is not my signature, nor do I know this mortuary. It may even be a vacant lot if you look it up on Google Earth. I'm going to go to the police as my father's remains are missing and have been stolen from this office. Can I have a copy of the security footage from when these fake mortuary people were in the building this morning?"

Jill had been prepared to deliver that very same speech to the clerk and said she was glad that Melanie took care of it. She doubted the ME's office would release security footage to them, but once they got the police involved they would no doubt view the footage themselves. She could feel the anxiety by the person trying to help them, and frankly the distress over the loss of Mr. Thomas's remains.

They left the building with the documentation in hand, and the clerk's name for the police. They drove to the police head-quarters, which was an ugly red brick building, and Jill asked for the detectives division after explaining their concerns. They were asked to wait while the receptionist checked to see if the detective they had an appointment with for later that day was available now, given the new developments. They waited about fifteen minutes and Jill was just beginning to think of a Plan B when a door opened and a man in a plain clothes outfit looked at the receptionist, who nodded at the three women.

The man walked over and introduced himself, "Hello, I'm Detective Elias Chambers; what can I do for you today?"

Melanie hesitated as though life had become too much for her so Jill stepped in and made introductions, "Hello Detective, I'm Dr. Jill Quint, a private Forensic Pathologist and private investi-gator hired by Melanie Thomas who is the daughter of Mr. Ed Thomas. We've just come from the Medical Examiner's Office and his remains were picked up from an unknown entity and are missing at this point. We originally had an appointment with you later today to discuss the suspicious autopsy results, and the fact that he had received threatening letters before his death. In addi-tion, his apartment was broken into by someone apparently looking for those threatening letters. We have the letters with us. And this is my assistant, Madison Lewis."

That was quite a story for Detective Chambers to take note of. There is a missing body, threatening documents, and an inconclusive autopsy by the ME's office. He also wondered who this private detective and forensic pathologist was.

"Ladies, let's see if I can get a conference room so we can discuss this further . . . just a moment please."

A short time later, they followed the detective into the elevator and up three stories, to where Jill guessed that the detective's office was nearby. He showed them into a room that was used for both meetings and interviewing people. Jill thought that because of a two-way mirror, likely on one side of the room. However, the furniture was a little nicer than expected when dealing with hardened criminals.

"Give me a moment to look at these materials," the detective said. The three women sat in silence, waiting as he read the medical examiner's report, the fake mortuary report, the threatening letters, and a video of the apartment in the condition they saw that morning before they began straightening it up.

"This is a first for me in my twenty-year police career. I've never been presented with a missing body. Here's a question for you, Dr. Quint: given the security measures at the Bureau of Printing and Engraving, how would anyone get something in there to kill Mr. Thomas that didn't affect the other employees?"

"I don't know. I haven't had a tour of the Department of Treasury to understand the layout there. However, poisoning is the oldest form of murder in the book, and for all we know, he could've come back from lunch or coffee break, having consumed something that wasn't agreeable. I was set to perform an autopsy later today, which I cannot do until we locate his remains."

After rubbing his face over the weirdness of the case, he began asking Melanie questions about herself and her father. A while later, he had a sense of who the players were in the case, and the depth of the weirdness. First thing he wanted to do was visit the medical examiner's office, and so he told his guests. He also entered into evidence the threatening letters that Jill had brought with her.

"There's a lot to unravel here. I'm going to start at the medical examiner's office and move on from there. I'm sure I will have to get special clearance to visit Mr. Thomas's workplace. Even though I'm a cop, they don't let just anybody walk in there."

"I'd like to go with you as a second set of eyes to both locations. I know your first instinct is to deny my request because you don't work with civilians, but look me up after we leave. I've been very helpful to both the American police and the FBI as well as internationally, and that's all I want to do here. Here's my business card with my cell phone number on it. Here's the cell phone number of the FBI Special Agent in Charge in San Francisco, if you need a reference," Jill said, writing Leticia Ortiz's information on the card.

Jill doubted the officer would take her along. As it was, he would have to get special permission to visit the Bureau and would have an armed guard. Furthermore, he was more likely to take someone from his department with him than her. But she could always make the request. He nodded after making sure he had all of Melanie's information and then escorted them out of the building.

"What do you think?" Melanie asked, as they walked to her car.

"Like many police officers, he was hard to read. However, if for no other reason than this is a unique case with your father's body missing, I think we have his time and attention," Jill said.

"So where should we go next?" Melanie asked.

"We need to talk to his co-workers. Have you ever met them?"

"No. In all my time with my father, very little time was spent with a third person."

"Okay, let's return to his apartment and see if we can find any information on his co-workers, but before that, let's return to the medical examiner's office and collect your father's possessions. Perhaps there was a cell phone in his pockets or something else that will give us a clue."

Melanie did as Jill suggested and headed back to the ME's office. They walked inside and presented themselves to collect her father's possessions. After a pause, Susan Rock Taylor again came out to chat with the three women.

"I'm sorry, Ms. Thomas, but the police requested we hold onto everything Mr. Thomas arrived with, so I can't release his possessions just yet."

"Has anyone found my father's body?"

"We're working on the problem, but no, we haven't found the funeral home that picked him up."

"Did they use a hearse?" Madison asked.

"No, our security film showed a sprinter van taking his remains away."

"Okay, thank you," Jill said.

Melanie wasn't sure where to go next.

"Let's go back to your father's apartment," Jill said.

Melanie nodded and they headed to her car and were soon back inside the apartment. When she'd unlocked the apartment this time, it didn't feel as bad given that they had made headway in straightening the place out. Madison looked for a place to dump spoiled food and was soon outside with a large trash bag. She felt like someone was watching her and she looked around, but didn't see anything. She turned around and studied what was nearby. She looked up to see if anyone was looking at her from an open window, but she still didn't see anything. Then she looked at the parked cars for anyone staring at her. She saw nothing, decided she was just being paranoid, and returned to the apartment to finish putting the kitchen to rights.

Jill pulled up her video of the apartment and took a look at the chaos when they first arrived to see if anything might strike her as being out of place or something she could explore. Their victim was apparently quite a music lover, as he had both a piano and two guitars. She looked at the bench for the piano and opened the lid to find more letters inside sheets of music. Apparently, the searchers hadn't known that piano benches often stored music. These letters looked to be originals and not copies of the one found in the freezer.

"Ladies, I found additional letters," Jill called out. "I wonder where your father found the letters? If they were mailed, you would have thought that he would have kept the envelopes."

Melanie returned to the living room and said, "He said that they reached him in a variety of ways. He found some in a pocket of a jacket or his backpack after riding the subway. He would arrive at work and discover a letter in his lunch sack. One time he arrived home from the grocery store and found a letter in his grocery bag."

"That's creepy," Madison said.

"Did he discuss contacting the police?" Jill asked.

"No. They have police at his workplace, so he contacted them," Melanie said.

"That makes sense. I've read a few of these letters and while they don't explicitly say what the threat was, we know of at least ten letters. I haven't lined them up in order even if I can figure that out, but either the threat was made to him in person or it was made in earlier letters which we don't have. It seems like we need to contact the police force at the Bureau and see if the first letter was given to them."

Melanie sat down on her father's sofa and put both hands to her head as though she was either in pain or thinking hard. Jill looked over at Madison, who shrugged.

Melanie looked up and said, "I'm trying to remember what my father said, and exact details when he told me about the letters."

"Do you remember why he thought they were threatening?" Jill asked.

"The letters had a lot of innuendo in them as you can see, but my father understood what the threat was. Something else was going on at that time, so we moved our conversation on. If only I had known the threat to his life by these letters, I would have done my best to get to the bottom of them."

"Hindsight is always 20/20. I would've thought if you had known there were so many letters, both you and your family would've pressured your father into getting more law enforcement involved in the case. I'm going to ask the Treasury's police force to look up what they did with his case. If I don't get anywhere, perhaps Detective Chambers can get the information from them."

Jill pulled out her cell phone to call the detective about the additional letters they had found. She wanted to know if he had an update on where Mr. Thomas's remains were. She had already forwarded him her standard form, indicating that she had the right to speak to him on behalf of the victim's next of kin.

"Detective, any update on our missing body? Also, we found additional letters in the apartment. They're similar to the ones we found in the chicken package."

"Dr. Quint, I've been bombarded between getting the background on you, and making sure your form satisfies the District's laws regarding next of kin. Where did you find the additional letters?"

"Call me Jill. I found them in the piano bench. He had a second compartment in the bench that must not have been discovered by the people who tossed his apartment. The letters are similar to the other ones in their threats and they're not specific about what exactly they wanted him to do. I'm wondering if he took the first letters to the Security department at the Department of the Treasury. It's hard to know what the original threat was that is referred to in subsequent letters."

"I can see you've been busy, Jill. I'm going to give his employer a call as that is part of the standard detective process. This case has been getting odder by the moment, and I'd like to see what his employer has to say."

"Can I go with you?" Jill asked the detective.

"Seriously? If you have been involved as much as your record says you have, you know I can't take you into an interview."

"I'd be happy to sign a 'no-cost to your department' contract so you can call me a civilian consultant," Jill offered, holding up her fingers in quote marks.

The detective sighed, and said, "That's just another complication I have to run down. You know I have superiors, right? I'm not the free agent you are to go where I want with this case."

"Detective, I do know that you can bring me on as a civilian consultant and given my credentials, there is a basis for me being a consultant. However, I'd rather at the moment you head to Ed Thomas's employer and interview them. I'd like to know what the original threat was, and it hasn't been described in any of the letters we've uncovered yet. Please call me or Melanie after you've finished with the results of that interview. Thank you," Jill said and then ended the call before he had the chance to argue with her.

"I don't know if I'll get anywhere with the detective, but it was worth a try. They still haven't found your father's remains. I should've asked about street cameras in the District. Let's just continue to put this apartment back to rights and see if we come across anything else. There's not a lot I can do without your father's remains and without access to the Bureau of Engraving security force."

Melanie nodded, and the three women went back to organizing the apartment. The day came to a close with no new information, and Jill was at an odd standstill. It was so rare that she was denied the opportunity to participate in an autopsy.

Madison and Jill said goodbye to Melanie and returned to their hotel. Once there, they brainstormed on how Jill's team might be used.

"Jo usually checks out the finances of everyone involved in the case. The only people we know about so far are Melanie and her father. I'll ask her to take a look at them and see if she sees anything off. I'll ask Marie to do her usual dossier on Melanie and her father. At this point, I think that's all we can do tonight."

Madison nodded and they dined together and returned to their rooms. Jill called Nathan to hear about his day, and that of her dog and his cat. He always took Arthur to work with him as he liked to be around the outside of Nathan's place of work. That left Trixie, Jill's dog, to roam her vineyard in the cat's absence.

CHAPTER 4

*J*ill was pleased when her cell phone rang before nine in the morning with the detective's name.

"It's Jill. What's up?"

"This case is getting more twisted by the moment. We have the traffic department tracking the fake mortuary vehicle. Unfortunately, it left the District and entered Virginia. We're having to work across state lines to locate its path."

"What are the odds of finding Mr. Thomas's remains?"

"I have no idea. Like I told you, I've never worked on a case with a stolen body. You have to admit it's pretty strange."

"I wonder if the plan all along was to steal the body, or once his daughter hired a detective, whoever caused his death, decided to get rid of the evidence?"

"That's pure speculation. Other than what we caught on camera, we have no evidence about this crime so far."

"What about the coroner's report? Did they find anything during their autopsy?"

"As you know, a lot of their toxicology tests take a while for results. At this point, there's no obvious cause of death," the detective said.

"How about the Treasury police or whatever they're called? Did they have the original letters that Mr. Thomas received?"

"Well, something strange is going on there. They have no record of any meetings taking place or any concerns voiced by Mr. Thomas. I would guess by their response that they're covering up something. They can't be that incompetent and Miss Thomas was pretty clear that her father had spoken to them and I don't doubt her about this."

"Were they surprised that his body was missing?"

"They were just surprised that I wanted to talk to them. I got no reaction about the missing body. It tells me something is wrong in that department."

"So your next steps are to work with your Virginia colleagues to see if you can get more video on where the car went. Toxicology results from the medical examiner will probably be two to three weeks. What are you going to do about your suspicions with the Treasury police?"

"I'm gonna talk to my lieutenant about the situation, as I am rather flummoxed with all the strangeness of this case. I don't suppose you have any other ideas?"

"Let me review the medical examiner's report. We don't know how he died at work, and if I read the report and look at the lab results, I can at least rule some things out."

"We know he didn't die by gunshot wound, or by stabbing or a beating."

"I think if I were you, I would ask to interview his co-workers, and also ask if they have cameras on the interior of the building. If you're creating millions of brand-new dollars every day, I have to think they have cameras watching the process to make sure the workers aren't walking away with hundred-dollar bills."

"I have to agree with you on those suggestions. I'll get back to you later today. What are you working on?" the detective asked out of curiosity. Since her expertise was in a dead body, and she didn't have one, nor did she have access to people who needed to be interviewed, how was she going to spend her day?

"I think I might've mentioned that I have a team that helps me with many of these cases. One of my people is a forensic accountant, so she's going to look into the finances of father and daughter. Another team member is what I call a social media maven, and she's also going to research father and daughter. So hopefully I'm going to get some new information from their work."

"You're investigating your client?"

"Yes. I had a man hire me for a case in Texas because his wife died while giving a speech at a medical convention. He was the actual murderer. So yes, I always look into the clients who hire me.

"I know you're dealing with two branches of government here —the federal government and the District government. Will your lieutenant be able to bring any pressure on this federal government agency to give you information on the case? You must frequently have cases that bridge both levels of government. Do you guys normally work cooperatively, or does each department act like a bureaucrat and refuse to share information?"

"Wow, you don't pull any punches. We've had success with cooperation in the past, and we've also had some terrible failures, and I have no idea which way this will go."

"I have friends in the federal government, and in particular the FBI, and I won't hesitate to use them to leverage a federal department. But I'd rather you have cooperation and start there," Jill said.

"That's good to know. In addition to all the problems in this case, I'd also hate to be putting out fires that you start locally."

"Detective, in my other life, I grow grapes and make wine, and my grapes are all the better for the honey delivered by the bees. That's my approach in life."

They finished their conversation and ended the call.

Jill had a call scheduled with her friends, Jo and Marie, to see what they found in regard to the case.

"So, Melanie didn't mention that her father provided her with start-up funding for her company, did he?" Jo asked.

"How much funding did he provide?" Jill asked.

"He provided $50,000. Which in the grand scheme of things isn't that much money and certainly not enough for most family members to kill their loved one over."

"How well has Melanie done with the company? Would she have been able to pay her father back in, say, five years?"

"She's been in business two years and I would say in another year she would've paid him back. Of course, we don't know what their arrangement was. Maybe they set up an agreement where he was a silent partner. I'd have to do a lot more research to figure that out."

"Where did he get the fifty thousand? Was it savings? Did he borrow against a pension?" Jill asked.

"I think he got a low-interest loan that he borrowed against his future pension. If she pays him back in three years, it was a good investment and something many parents would do for their child."

"How about Mr. Thomas? Other than that loan payment, how are his finances? What kind of assets did he have?" Jill asked.

"He was a hard-working guy. He had future military and government pensions when he turned sixty-five. He was saving money each year. Other than a car, he had no other assets. He didn't own a home, a boat, or vacant land."

"Was he making alimony payments?"

"No. Melanie's parents never married, so there never would have been alimony. Melanie's mother works and earns a higher salary than her father. She discovered her father about the time that child support payments would have stopped."

"Anything else you need to tell me about it?" Jill asked.

"Not that I can think of."

"Marie, what do you have?"

"I've just scratched the surface. Mr. Thomas has an honorable discharge from the military. He seems mostly a happy-go-lucky guy. I couldn't find anything nasty that he said on the Internet and he doesn't follow any strange groups. He largely stays out of the fray of the world."

"So your summary would be to hire him."

"Yes, and I would even say that about his daughter. She also doesn't say rude things about people in public that I could find. She has a degree from the University of Maryland and is just an average person going about her life. She posted a few pictures with her father, but she never announced when they had met, which was a good thing to keep off of social media, so points to her for that. Like Jo, I'll keep looking, but so far, they both have pretty clean records, and I would recommend hiring them both."

In the end, there wasn't new information for Jill to act on. She was happy for her client's sake that there were no red flags there.

She got a call from the detective about two hours later. Apparently the people who had stolen Mr. Thomas's body were lazy. They dumped the body bag with him in it along the roadside in Virginia. Someone cleaning up highway litter found it and called the police. The body was on its way to the District's coroner's office. As there were remains, and were now part of a new crime, the medical examiner would need to take a second look at the body. The detective had gotten an invite for Jill to join him in observing the autopsy. Jill raised her hands in the air in a sign of victory and gave a high five to Madison.

"I'm sorry that you can't join me at this time, but you lack the credentials for the police to take you seriously yet. Based on what I see at the M.E.'s office, I may still do my own autopsy on the body and you will be able to observe that."

"Call me weak, but I think I'd rather not see a body that's been cared for in the manner of Mr. Thomas's. I hope they didn't shove it out of the vehicle while it was moving. I'd hate to have his head break off his body or something equally gross."

"I suppose that's possible, but in over a thousand autopsies, I haven't seen that problem yet. Fingers crossed that that didn't happen to Melanie's father. If it did happen, that would be difficult for an open casket."

Jill contacted Melanie to give her an update.

"Hi, Melanie, this is Jill. The police have located your father's remains. I've been invited to join the detective as the medical examiner reviews his remains. It is a separate crime to steal a body, and then leave it by the roadside in Virginia, so they will be collecting evidence on that second crime."

When Jill heard snuffling on the other side of the phone, she felt bad about her word choice when talking to Melanie. Then Melanie spoke.

"I've tried not to shed any tears over my father's death, and these are just angry tears, but how dare they treat my father that way! You've got to find out who's behind all of this. It was bad enough that they murdered him well before his time, but then to be so disrespectful of his remains makes me so mad."

Jill could hear Melanie blow her nose and when she was done she said, "I'm sorry about that too, Melanie. You should know that the medical examiner will be very respectful with your father's remains and they'll make sure that your designated mortuary will be the ones picking him up this time. A mistake like this happens once in a lifetime in a medical examiner's office. They may have five to ten bodies a day picked up. They may think they have all the right paperwork. They made a mistake in this case and they'll never repeat it again. Would you like me to call you later tonight with what I found at the M.E.'s office? It may be late."

"I don't care if it's two o'clock in the morning, call me."

"Also, Melanie, depending on what I see in here tonight, I may want to perform a private autopsy at the mortuary. I'm hopeful that all of my questions will be answered and we don't have to delay his funeral services."

"Do what you need to do to make sure you collect any evidence that's needed to convict the people who did this."

Jill exchanged more sympathies with Melanie and they soon ended the call.

Madison listened to the conversation and said, "When you invited me in on this investigation, it sounded pretty routine, but it has quickly become strange. Is that the usual sequence of an investigation?"

Jill thought for a few moments and then said, "Maybe that happens about a third of the time. People actually die from old age, heart disease, cancer, and diabetes, and that's easily confirmed by any coroner. Sometimes I just do a paper review for a family and charge a small fee for that investigation and explanation. Usually the person who died was hiding some of their medical problems and the family members were trying hard to ignore some obvious symptoms. That's how some families deal with serious illnesses."

"It's kind of sad, but I get it. I won't get those kinds of cases as I'm not going to medical school to get your kinds of qualification in this lifetime. I'll just refer those cases to you."

"Almost all of my work comes about because someone is looking for help understanding a death. Then that spills into an investigation. Once you establish yourself, you may want to subcontract to me the autopsy part and keep the detective work for yourself."

"You would allow that?" Madison asked.

"Of course. I'm in this profession to bring truth to families. Whether I do that because a family contacted me directly or you hire my services makes no difference to me. In time you may find someone closer to your home to replace me and that's fine, too. I have enough business and a winery to run, so my plate is full.

Also, my team has daytime jobs and I can't have them full time, and they're just as important as I am to resolving each case."

"That's something else I'll have to build is a team like yours."

"If you don't have friends in HR and finance, I would look at your father's company as he likely has those resources. For a fee, I'm sure Jo and Marie could evaluate them or train them."

Madison nodded and wrote stuff in a notebook that she was using. It contained her hours of training under Jill, things she needed to think of when setting up her business, and a third section she called *ways to think about investigations*. It was a mouthful, but Jill liked the idea because thinking was the skill she brought to any investigation.

Jill stood up and said, "I need to grab a taxi to get to the medical examiner's office. I'll email you any findings."

Jill met Detective Chambers in front of the DC Medical Examiner Office. They were buzzed in and taken to the autopsy area. Jill met the medical examiner in charge of this autopsy. It was a different physician than had initially examined Mr. Thomas.

"Hello Detective, Dr. Quint. We received some interesting information from Mr. Thomas's initial autopsy. His intestines contained remains of his meal the night before which we sent out for analysis and it tested positive for ricin."

"Wow," replied the detective and Jill simultaneously. Jill added, "He was lucky to make it to work that morning, or unlucky if that's not how you want to spend your last minutes alive."

"Yes."

"So we have a homicide, and that was before the remains were stolen from your office," Chambers said.

"So it would seem. Shall we head into the room and begin this second autopsy?"

Jill followed the detective and pathologist into a typical autopsy room. She was pleased to see that Mr. Thomas appeared to be intact with no additional marks, at least to his face, from his time in the Virginia countryside.

"I'm training someone new in private detection, and she wondered if his head might have bounced off his body if they tossed his body out of a moving vehicle. Logically, I don't think that can happen, and I'm glad to see that it did not."

"I agree with your trainee, Dr. Quint. That is an interesting proposition. I would think it would take significant force to decapitate a head from a dead body. Hopefully, I'll never see the answer to that question in my career."

They proceeded with the autopsy, finding nothing unusual. The remains appeared to be uninjured from their time spent in the wilderness. The finding of ricin in the stomach contents confirmed the cause of death. Ricin interfered with the manufacturing of proteins at the cellular level. So cells would start to die off throughout the body once they no longer had the protein to function. Death occurs when enough of the cells of the major organs die. Mr. Thomas was likely not feeling great when he arrived at work the morning of his death.

An hour later, the procedure was done, and the detective and Jill were changing back into street clothes. They thanked the medical examiner for her time and exited the building.

"Detective, I'll be talking with Melanie tonight, but I'd like you to call her first given the autopsy finding of ricin."

"Yes, I can do that. I'll begin with tracking the source of the Chinese food. Maybe we will look around and there will be camera footage that gives us our suspect."

"Yeah, good luck with that," Jill said, and they parted ways. She drove back to the hotel and quickly updated Madison with the new information. Then she called Melanie, figuring the detective had had enough time to talk with her.

"Hi, Melanie. I presume you've already talked to Detective Chambers?"

"Yes, and I gave him the name of the Chinese restaurant that Dad routinely ordered from. In my experience, Dad ordered from that restaurant on the same day each week. Any bad guy wanting to do him harm could pick that location and do exactly what they did."

"It's a good thing you didn't share the food with your father, or you would likely be dead too. It is such a deadly poison. It takes so little to kill humans and it's easy to hide in food."

"I know. I thought about that as I have shared food from that restaurant with Dad in the past."

"So, Melanie, you have a decision to make about your father's case. It's clearly a homicide and the police are on the case. You can end my services right now, or I can continue working for you privately. It's your call."

"I have the money to pay for your services for two weeks. I want to keep you on board as things seem to happen around you. While I have faith in Detective Chambers, I feel like I've gotten more information quickly because of your presence."

"Thank you, Melanie. I will do my best for your father. My team is working on different aspects of this case, and hopefully I'll have some new information for you tomorrow morning. I hope you get some rest now that you know where your father's remains are, and that they suffered no harm while out in the wilderness."

"Yeah, I have a funeral to plan. I couldn't do that until we located him. Good night, Jill."

They wrapped up the call, and Jill returned to her conversation with Madison and her plan for how to find Mr. Thomas's murderer.

"You need to get into his work site, and I have to think you'll need the detective to get you in there," Madison said.

"Yes, I will need his help. I think I'll also try to visit the part that's open to the public. We may be able to visualize the murder scene. However, I also want to talk to his co-workers and the security folks at the Bureau. They definitely won't talk to me, and I wouldn't be surprised if they put roadblocks up. I seem to remember that our victim thought the Bureau's security force was in on the threatening letters. If so, they're going to do everything possible to block us from getting information. Then again, I've had a lack of cooperation on many other cases, and you should expect this problem when you set up your own agency, Madison."

"The fact that you're a medical doctor makes it hard for all kinds of people to ignore you. I won't have that advantage."

"What you could do is take a job as a coroner in a small town somewhere in the United States. There are cities and counties where the coroner is elected and not someone with a medical background."

"I might just do that. I don't want to be ineffective on the job because people don't take me seriously."

"True, but given your youth and your gender, many people in positions of authority won't take you seriously and you'll have to fight for answers. So, take a boxing class while you're at it," Jill said with a grin. "In time, you'll develop connections to law enforcement that can serve as a reference for you or get you help when the going gets tough. I made friends early on with an FBI Special Agent in Charge of the San Francisco office. She connected me to her fellow agents in other parts of the US and internationally. She's been a wonderful reference."

"That's good advice in many ways. In what kind of investigation did you meet?"

"An international sniper wanted by Interpol was trying to take me down. I wouldn't wish that on you. My dog saved my life initially and then the FBI finished her off along with a couple of police agencies."

"I'd like to wait for that kind of excitement until I'm at least in my thirties."

"You're probably going to be stuck with a bunch of boring surveillance cases for a few years. That's fine as you build your competence and team to handle scarier stuff. Now, back to Mr. Thomas. Let's put together a list of questions to ask his employer and co-workers. If the detective gets inside and agrees to take me with him, I feel like we'll only have one chance to interview these people. So let's make a list."

They spent the remainder of the evening compiling questions. Before Jill and the detective had parted at the medical examiner's office, she had made a plea for him to take her with him inside the Bureau of Printing and Engraving. She listed her reasons and some options for the detective to legitimize her. She sent him a file with the various law-enforcement agencies she worked with worldwide and the cases she'd helped those agencies to close. While she wasn't a member of the force, Jill had street cred for her prior work in a crime lab as well as her cooperation with so many agencies. Still, it was the detective's decision and she could only hope that her body of work swayed him. After her nightly call with Nathan, she settled down to sleep.

When she awoke the next morning, she had an email from the detective. It stated that he'd gotten a search order approved by a judge. Furthermore, Jill could join him as a member of the "crime scene team." Her opinion of the detective was increasing; including her was a major win for her and Mr. Thomas. She was glad he recognized her resourcefulness. She was to meet him at his office at nine and they would drive to the Bureau with two other members of his office. She had breakfast with Madison and they went over their questions one more time, and then she was off to meet the detective. She assigned Madison the task of following up on the ricin-laden Chinese food in her absence.

CHAPTER 5

Jill entered the building housing Detective Chambers and the other detectives. When she arrived, she saw that he had a badge and an ugly, unisex white paper jumpsuit for her to wear, along with a mask and hair net which would comfortably hide her features. They would have to log in to Security at the Bureau and they would be scanned before and after. She was given a crime scene tackle box to carry and they had a discussion about who would do what. Jill would partner with the detective. They had a search warrant for the workspace, Mr. Thomas's locker, and the lounge, and to interview his co-workers and the security force. As it was a federal building, they had to get a federal judge to approve the search. The stolen remains and the autopsy results of ricin poison facilitated making the judge quick to sign a warrant. With everyone's roles established, they left in several vehicles. It was a slow drive through the most congested part of the capital.

They parked their vehicles on a side street and headed for the front door. There was a guard inside the door, and the doors were locked. The guard motioned them to the visitor entrance. Detective Chambers stepped up and put his badge to the door along with the search warrant. He sent someone back to the patrol car to get the log they used to break down doors. The guard was on his walkie-talkie and held up his hand. The detective looked at his watch and held up two fingers. Meaning the guard had two minutes to open the door or they would force their way in. Jill was happy to have a mask on because she was enjoying the discomfort of the guard. He arrived at work that day thinking he would be directing visitors to another entrance, and instead he was confronted by the police and a threat to break down the door.

Jill had checked her watch to see what would happen when the two minutes were up. Fortunately she didn't have to find out. Just about the time the detective was about to motion that the door be broken, a second guard arrived.

He unlocked the door and said, "Officer, you need to go around to the visitors' entrance," and he moved to shut the door.

The detective held up the search warrant again, and said, "You are under a court order to open the door to give us access to the employee area. We won't be wasting our time sorting ourselves through the visitor entrance. We have a murder investigation under way, and we need access to the Bureau for a search. If you do not allow us in, we'll break into your building and you will be arrested for ignoring a search warrant. Do you understand?"

"Officer, it's against the Bureau's policy to let anyone in this entrance other than an employee. Employees have gone through a security and background check. You have not."

"It's Detective, and it doesn't matter what your policy is. You are under a court order to let us in. I'm going to arrest you for obstructing justice if you continue to try and bar our way into the employee area. Or you can invite me and my team inside while you rustle up additional security officers to observe us while we search specific places inside this building."

"Just a minute, Detective. This is highly unusual. Let me get additional officers in place. It may take ten to fifteen minutes."

"We are not waiting ten to fifteen minutes. I'll have you

arrested and on your way to the DC jail. I don't care if you have to pull people from the administrative offices, but we're going to be moving through your facility to the areas we need to search. It's all here in the search warrant and you can keep that copy if you need to. Let's start with your employee break room or locker room. We need to get into Mr. Ed Thomas's locker and then we need to examine the area that he worked in, which I believe is a machine that cuts sheets of paper into dollar bills."

The detective moved to push the guard aside, and enter whatever was behind the door that he had come through to confront them.

"Wait a minute, wait a minute; we're all officers of the law here. What's the rush?"

Detective Chalmers looked at the man's employee ID picture and said, "My team are officers of the law, I don't know what you are. I don't know if you're a private contractor, but I doubt you've been through the Police Academy or have any detective experience, or you wouldn't be asking me such stupid questions. A search warrant is best served as a surprise. Now unlock that door behind you or you're going to be in handcuffs pretty soon." The detective followed through by reaching behind him to grab a pair of handcuffs snapped onto his belt.

The security guard sighed and opened the door while talking on the walkie-talkie.

"All units, if available, please come to the employee entrance. The police are here attempting to serve a search warrant."

Jill was sure that the detective was smirking behind his mask. The entire team was likely grateful to be hiding any number of facial expressions. After more posturing by the Bureau's security force, they shortly arrived at an employee locker room.

"Which locker belonged to Mr. Ed Thomas?" the detective asked.

They looked around the room, but there were no names on

any of the gray lockers. There were stickers on a few, and a variety of locks.

"I don't know. As you can see, there are no employee names on any of the lockers."

"Okay then, you can either call personnel and find out which locker was assigned to Ed Thomas or my team and I will cut all the locks off until we find his locker."

"Just a moment."

The guard was giving them very dirty looks, but he was reluctantly cooperating. He wasn't anxious to have handcuffs placed around his wrist and sent to jail for a few hours.

Additional resources arrived at the employee lounge. When the guard was assured that he had enough people to watch the detective's team, he called someone to see if he could find the locker number of Mr. Thomas. About a minute later, he ended the call and said, "It's number 65."

The detective and his team approached that locker and pulled out what looked to be landscape trimmers, but these were for cutting through steel locks. A short time later the lock was broken open and the locker opened. They put everything into a bag and labeled it and were done in under five minutes.

The detective looked around to see if there were any surveillance cameras in this room. He didn't see any but still, he asked.

"I don't see any surveillance cameras in this area. Can you confirm that?"

The guard replied, "No cameras here."

"Okay, show us the workstation of Mr. Thomas. I would appreciate it if you would show me where the cameras are located between here and where he was found on the ground."

"I need your team to walk single file, so we can keep a visual on everybody's hands."

The detective didn't trust the guard to give him correct information and so he directed his team to also look for cameras as they passed through the hallways of the Bureau of Engraving. They would pause for a moment and look each time someone pointed out a camera. Each time the guard said nothing. The detective gave him a stink eye.

"See, this is why you're not a member of the same law-enforcement community that I am, because if you were, you would cooperate with us on this murder investigation. Instead, you're doing your best to hamper our investigation."

Soon they arrived at the cutting machine. It was a noisy environment, and the workers wore earplugs. The detective paused and looked around for cameras. Then he told the guard that he wanted to interview the employee who was operating the machine.

The guard nodded and approached the employee, who turned the machine off. It was still a noisy area as other printing presses and stacking machines were operating.

The detective held out his badge to the employee and said, "Hi, I'm Detective Chambers from District PD and we have a court order to interview you and other co-workers of Mr. Thomas. Do you have any questions for me before we start?"

"Do I need an attorney to answer your questions?" the employee asked. Then he looked over at the guard and said, "Should someone from HR be here?"

"We just want to question you about anything Mr. Thomas said on the job and a little bit about this machine you're operating. Unless you hired someone to murder Mr. Thomas, you have nothing to worry about."

"I've worked with Ed for over fifteen years; I would never think of hurting him. He's a really good guy. He didn't mind training you on new equipment. He rarely took time off work, and on occasion, when we had lunch together, he always had something kind to say about someone. I really miss him."

The detective led him through a series of questions, but in Jill's estimation, there was no new information. Pretty much all of his co-workers said the same thing. So Detective Chambers moved on to the guard.

"Can you take me to wherever your department is headquartered? I have questions for your leaders and I want to see the cameras that are on the interior of this building."

The sound of the cutting machine resumed as they followed the guard out of the area. They traveled through some hallways, and again the guards stopped and pointed at a room with a lot of television screens. Jill decided she was glad she wasn't in charge of security for this building. It seemed like you were constantly fighting against an unknown bank robber with all the money lying around as it was being made, compiled, and shipped. If an employee could make off with a pallet of fresh bills, they wouldn't need to work the rest of their life. The detective took a minute to study the various camera angles. He located the one that was focused on the area where Mr. Thomas had crumpled to the ground. He made a note to get a copy of the tape from the day that he collapsed.

From there they were shown into a small meeting room, and some new people filed in. Jill guessed from their names that these were the management representatives in charge of keeping all of those millions of dollars safe.

The detective shared the search warrant with the men, and then began to ask questions.

"I understand that Mr. Thomas alerted you to some threatening letters he was receiving. I would like to see the materials relating to the investigation that you carried out to verify his complaint."

Two of the men gave a quick glance at each other, and then one of them said, "We don't have any record of meeting with him regarding any threats."

"Do you have a record of ever meeting with Mr. Thomas during his 20+ years of employment?"

"No, it's just as his co-workers said; he was a pleasant guy who had no problems on the job."

The questioning went on for a while longer, but the detective gained no new information. He submitted a request for the tapes around the time of their victim's death. It had taken quite an effort to get inside the building, and he didn't want to leave without having all of his questions answered. However, given all the roadblocks, he had not gained much new information in the search other than to confirm that whatever was going on in the Bureau of Printing and Engraving, the security force clearly was in on it.

After returning to Detective Chambers' department, they chatted a little bit about what they observed at the Bureau.

"I thought the security guys were over the top with distrust and throwing roadblocks in our way. However, I'm not sure how I would've reacted, knowing how much money is at stake in that place. At least they called HR and got the locker number for our victim. I think our visit would've been even uglier if we had had to break into every locker," Jill said.

"Yes, I don't disagree with your assessment. That was the first time I've been inside that building and for all their security force knows, our search warrant could've been a fake document and we could've been fake police officers. That said, I wasn't going to give them advance notice. I think they still could've hidden things from us, but they didn't have much time. It was interesting that they denied that Mr. Thomas had brought the threatening letters to their attention. Either the guy truly wasn't in the know, or we were lied to, and I don't know which one it is."

The crime scene technicians spilled the contents of their victim's locker onto the conference room table. Wearing gloves, they sorted through the items. There were pictures of his daughter, a few protein bars, and various bits of paper. They examined the papers page by page and found nothing of interest.

"Do you think the interviews of his co-workers yielded any new information?" Jill asked.

"I don't think so. I don't think he confided in his co-workers about the letters. I think he quickly got paranoid about who he could trust after his experience of dealing with his own internal resources. So I think the interviews with the co-workers were a bust," Chambers said.

"I would have to agree with your assessment, Detective. Other than potentially identifying who might be in on the threatening letters that our victim received, the search seemed a waste of time," Jill said.

"We dusted the body bag that held our victim in the Virginia countryside. The trouble with that is we have to eliminate the employees of the medical examiner's office—people who had the right to touch that bag. We also dusted the letters. Jill, can you confirm that you, your associate, and the victim's daughter all wore gloves?"

"Yes, I handed them out when we first arrived in the apartment. I knew my two helpers would not possibly know whether something was important enough to put gloves on for, so I asked that they wear them the entire time. I had my associate change her gloves as soon as she discovered the baggie holding the letters in the chicken as I didn't want her food soiled gloved hands to contaminate the letters. "

"I'm going to put in another search warrant to get the videotapes around the workstation of our victim. Unfortunately, I don't think that those tapes will yield anything as he was poisoned the night before. What I would love to have is the date he is alleged to have met with the security people about the threatening letters. I think I'll call the daughter and see if she can give us any specific dates. A judge may or may not sign off on that request."

"I want to thank you, Detective, for including me in the search of the victim's workplace. I'm going to return to my hotel now and see if my colleagues have gathered any interesting information on the parties involved. I asked Madison to run down the Chinese food source before I left this morning and that may present us with a clue. In this case, we have a likely motive, but we don't know who the person is with the motive. Do you have a report on the fingerprints lifted from the letters we located inside the victim's house?"

"We should have something back, let me pull that up." So saying, the detective tapped away on a few keys on his laptop and then stopped to read something. Then he looked up and replied, "The victim's prints were on the paper, but no other legible ones. If he met with anyone in the security force, they likely kept the letters rather than returning them to him, so we have no evidence from those. We tried to find the discarded Chinese food container, but he must have taken them out to the main trash dumpster which was emptied the day of his death."

"Or the guys that trashed his apartment were there for the takeout food containers. Okay, thanks," Jill said, getting up to leave. She had some research ideas she wanted to follow up on. So far they had no clue as to who had been threatening Ed Thomas. The letters were, of course, unsigned. They were a little wacky, though, as there were so many of them. Who writes letters full of threats nowadays? It appeared that there were at least ten—nine found at his residence and at least one that he shared with the security force. They weren't dated, so Jill had no idea over what period of time the letters were flowing. Also, someone was tailing their victim to be able to deposit so many letters into his possessions. Melanie said that her father commuted to work on the subway. She wanted to ride his path to understand where the letters might have been dropped. Rather than take a taxi back to her hotel, she searched for the nearest metro station and found herself back at their victim's apartment. She then walked to the metro and changed trains at a station before getting off near the Bureau. That piece of research completed, she headed back to the hotel after texting Madison her plans for the day.

CHAPTER 6

"What did you find out about the Chinese restaurant?" Jill asked.

"He was a regular patron. He ordered takeout on the same day every week for years."

"Was it the same entree?"

"No. Mr. Thomas had a copy of their menu and would order something different each week."

"Did he pick it up or have it delivered?"

"Initially he picked it up, but maybe two years ago he began using a ride-share service to deliver his food. On the night of his last order, two rideshares arrived to take care of his food. The owner didn't think anything of it at the time as it occasionally happened. So I assume the one that got there first was the murderer."

"The guy arrived before the food was finished cooking and the moment they had it bagged, he took off. Less than a minute later, the other driver walked in looking for the meal," Madison said.

"So my guess is our victim was under surveillance during the time he was receiving letters and his established eating pattern got him killed. Did the eatery have any surveillance video?"

"They have a camera aimed over the cash register, but the man stayed out of range and had a hoodie on. The owner remembered the man as it was unusual to have order confusion and said he was likely white and between the age of twenty-five and fifty. He said he was not good at judging people's ages—especially people who were a different race than his."

"The detective said there are no fingerprints on the letters other than our victim's. So that's a dead-end at the moment." Jill said.

"What kind of person writes these kinds of letters? I don't get it."

"What do you mean? I would say that they're psychos. Imagine the time it takes to sit down and write different letters. Furthermore, to be so sure that Mr. Thomas would be willing to print currency and no one would notice? Sounds like someone who is out of touch with the world," Jill said.

"Exactly. This is somebody who's not thinking about the bigger picture. They just have blinders on that allow them to only see what they want and need. Why does someone want currency that is worthless? Any retail clerk or bank employee would refuse the bills. It's like if you ask the Bureau of Printing and Engraving to make Monopoly money, then it's legitimate."

Jill's cell phone rang and it was Melanie Thomas.

"Hi Melanie."

"Hey, Jill. My father's phone was returned to me and I've been going through it. There's a picture of another letter and I think it's the one that he took to Security. We didn't find it in his apartment. The threats are explicit. The person or persons writing these letters are insurrectionists who think they need a new currency to go with their new government."

"Huh?" Jill said. This reasoning in the letter wasn't on her top fifty reasons to kill Mr. Thomas.

"I'll send you a copy now and then call me back."

Jill waited for the email to arrive on her laptop and then she and Madison read it. She immediately sent a copy to the detective, then called Melanie.

"Wow, Melanie, thanks for going through your father's phone. I'm sure that was difficult. It appears that the letter writer is someone your father served with in the military, but didn't stay in contact with much beyond the first year they left the military."

"Dad never mentioned any buddies from his military service. In fact, he didn't talk much about that time at all. I'll go through his apartment again as I think he had his military service stuff in a single box. He saved his uniform for a while, but then sold it or discarded it. I think he saved a few things—medals, certificates, pictures. He shared the Honorable Discharge certificate with me."

"Would you like some help with that?"

"No, I've been spending time there every day taking care of his stuff. I'll go over there now and see what I can find and send you anything."

"Okay. I'd especially be interested in any pictures he saved. I sent the letter to the detective and I'll give him a call now. I'm also going to have my team work on this insurrectionist group."

While Jill was speaking to Melanie, Madison had been searching for information on the group. Jill ended the call with her client and paused before dialing the detective.

"Do you have any information before I call the detective?"

"I do. I've been furiously taking notes on what I found—here, you can read and share."

Jill read the notes on Madison's tablet and nodded, "That's good and quick research. Thank you."

Jill thought for a millisecond about giving Madison more feedback, but she really owed the detective a call. It was getting late in the afternoon and she assumed he went home every night at some point.

"Chambers."

"Hi Detective, it's Jill Quint and I have new information for you. Is this a good time?"

"No, but lay it on me. What do you have?"

Jill discussed her findings with the detective including forwarding the letter from the victim's phone.

"I'm going to have to discuss this with my lieutenant. We didn't find the letter as I didn't have a search warrant for the phone. We debated fingerprinting the phone, but didn't see any value there. I'm glad the daughter found this letter. I'll give you a call later."

The call ended and Jill wondered if the detective meant that he would call her back in an hour, later today, or sometime in the future. She shrugged and decided it was time to call in the big guns. Jill had saved money in her business account for a time just like this. She didn't think the client could afford Jill's entire team, but she wanted their help.

"Can you use your father's connections to get us additional rooms at a cheap price? I'd like to bring my teammates here for the weekend and I need two additional hotel rooms at a reasonable price. It's coming out of my pocket, not the client's. Not that I would waste client money, I just think this case is getting freaking complicated."

Madison began working on her family's connections. Meanwhile Jill sent a text to Marie, Jo, and Angela to see if they could travel east for the weekend. A moment later she got a text back and she smiled, raising her hands in the air.

"Yeah! Turns out my good friend Henrik was visiting Wisconsin for a convention. He has a private plane and will drop everyone off tonight and transport them back on Sunday! I'll have their help for a three day weekend. Do you have lodging for us?"

"I do. My father has a friend who has a large empty condo here that we can all move to. It has six bedrooms. Maybe the money you save for your hotel can be money you pay your friends."

"That sounds like a plan, but I'll run it by Melanie. I never want to be untruthful with what my agency charges a client."

Jill did that and Melanie was okay and actually pleased that Jill was getting more help for the same amount of money spent.

"Let's pack and move, then we'll continue our research."

Another hour passed and they were ensconced in a luxury condo. Jill's friends would be arriving at the condo around nine that evening. After exploring the kitchen, they ordered a grocery delivery to supply them for the weekend.

"Did your father say how long we can use this space? Do I need to move back to a hotel on Monday?"

"We can use it for two weeks, so we're good."

Jill nodded and they returned to researching the insurrectionists. There was no news from the detective and as they included salads in their grocery delivery, they munched them while they worked. Jill wasn't sure if Henrik was coming, but if he was, he was a master phone security cracker and so she had Melanie deliver the phone to her just in case. They had the unlock code to it, but he might discover something in the phone they missed. She had a nice bottle of red wine breathing for her friends' arrival as well as some snacks.

They texted her their ETA as they entered the taxi that would bring them to the house. Jill was waiting outside for her friends' arrival, snuggled in a coat against the cool fall night. The taxi arrived and her three friends piled out with hugs all around. They entered the building, selected bedrooms, settled in, and returned to the dining room where Madison and Jill had set up her murder board. After handing out glasses of wine to everyone, Jill took them through what they had on the case so far.

"Insurrectionists? Wow, that's a new one for you, Jill. We've battled bad cops, the mafia, criminals wanted by Interpol, but never this group before," Marie said.

"What is even more bizarre is that they thought they could just have their friend print their new currency. Just because you print money doesn't mean it's useful anywhere. Did they have their own plates and just wanted the paper and the ink from the Bureau of Printing and Engraving?" Jo asked.

"Madison and I haven't figured that out. We were wondering what these people were thinking. If they didn't look like normal dollar bills, then they're just printing Monopoly money and there isn't a retail place anywhere in the world that would allow them to spend the money. It's like they thought they were going back to the Civil War, and they were the South and needed their own currency," Jill said.

"I'll do a deep dive into their social media stuff. Madison, why don't you join me as this is really important for you to learn in your future career," Marie said.

"I was discussing earlier with Madison that she should find her own local resources, but likely for a price you guys could train her associates to do some of what you do. You've been invaluable to my investigations, and I adore your company."

"Jill, what would you like me to do?" Angela asked. "Somehow I don't think it would do us any good if I went outside to a bar and photographed random people. That works in a lot of our cases, but it won't work in this one."

"The victim's daughter gave me his cell phone and his code to unlock it. If you could take a look at the pictures around a certain time and identify people, that would help. Also, I asked her to look through his old military stuff for photographs. She sent a couple of those over and I think someone in one of those photographs will be our insurrectionist. It's clear from the first threatening letter that they knew each other from military service two decades ago."

Angela nodded and went to work. That left Jo to investigate this group. "Let's start by looking at other groups of people who have tried to overturn the American government. Where did their funding come from? Our victim was followed to work and to the restaurant by someone from this group. A single person couldn't have followed him around the clock, so this group has resources."

Jo nodded and went to work. It was quiet in the condominium, except for the collection of keyboard sounds. Jill loved how her friends were so willing to spend the weekend with her doing research, nothing more than research. Of course, they had visited DC in the past and sampled its delights; still, she was lucky to have these friends.

After about an hour's work, Jill was flagging as it had been a long day. Also, she was a morning person, and she got progressively dumber as midnight approached.

She stood up and stretched and said, "I know I made you guys come here, and now I want to go to bed, but I was up early for a search at the Bureau of Printing and Engraving, and that was after an evening autopsy last night. Feel free to join me in slumber. Otherwise, I'll see you in the morning."

Her friends nodded and returned to their work. Jill was glad it was keeping them entertained.

She entered her bedroom, changed into her night clothes, and called Nathan before falling asleep. He was bummed that he wasn't there to help her. She reminded him that the only reason her friends were there was that ever-helpful Henrik and his private plane had conveniently been located close to them. They talked a little longer and Nathan realized Jill needed her brain to sleep and they said good night.

CHAPTER 7

*J*ill was up before everybody else the next morning, and looked to see if anyone had left her information to act on, but she saw none. Madison soon joined her, so she was able to question her as to whether they discovered anything the previous night after Jill had gone to bed.

"Any news? Did Marie or Jo find anything last night?"

"No, I worked with Marie. I'm researching groups focused on overthrowing the government, and it takes some time. They're not on the mainstream apps, so first you have to search for an app that contains their conversation. Then you have to set up your own account, so you can search for the relevant conversations. I felt slimy after reading some of the stuff. Some of these people are such idiots. They want to overthrow the government, but they have no plan. Like they want to abolish taxes, but still have some government services like the military. All I'll say is they're not the sharpest tools in the shed."

"That's always been my impression. Were they all on one social media platform or did you have to focus on several?" Jill asked.

"They are on a couple of platforms, and so we created accounts on all of them. I learned so much watching Marie navigate the waters, so to speak."

"Do you have any names? Did anyone say in any of these talk rooms that they were having some dude at the Bureau print money for them?"

"It took a lot of effort to find these accounts for these chat rooms. You have to apply to join them. So that was where we left it last night. We're waiting for an admin to approve our entry into some of these strange chat rooms."

"OK. Did Angela say if she had found anything?"

"Good morning," Angela said, approaching the dining room from the hallway that contained their bedrooms.

"Good morning! There's a tea kettle on the stove and I got some tea for you yesterday."

"Thank you. I'll make myself a cup, and I'll wake up and then answer your question about photos."

Jill smiled and waited for her friend to acclimate to the morning. She knew that Marie would wake up next, and Jo would come last. It had been their pattern over the last two decades of friendship. Jill was the extreme morning person, followed by Angela, then Marie, then Jo; it was part of a ritual for them as friends.

Jill returned to her conversation with Madison. "Did Jo find any sources of funding for any of these groups?"

"I don't think so. She was pounding away on the keyboard, and then noticed that Angela and Marie were retiring to the rooms, and she walked away mid-keystroke."

"I didn't think it would be that easy. I didn't think my friends would arrive and within an hour the case would be solved. However, I live in hope with each new case that it will be solved quickly."

"Yeah, you have a few deadlines here. You have your friends for a few days to help you in person, and then Melanie indicated she could pay for your services a few days beyond that. It seems like a tall order to solve this complex case within the next six days or so."

"There's a time limit on many of my cases. Sometimes it's because we're on vacation and we have tickets to return home. Other times, it's because someone is trying to kill us and so it's imperative that we solve the case or die. I think it is much the same for law enforcement. You have a multitude of clues and evidence to chase down at the beginning of the case. If you don't solve it within, say, those first two or three weeks, the case is likely to become a cold case."

"Yikes, it's a good thing my father isn't around to hear that comment; he might decide not to fund my future career. You all seem so mild mannered and low-key and that makes the job feel like it is a low-stress occupation," Madison said.

"What you see is what we are in real life. When you start hiring your employees, don't hire anyone high-strung as it makes the difficult cases worse. Seriously, though, I was offering a second opinion for a couple of years before it got dangerous."

Madison nodded and Angela pulled out a few photos to chat about.

"So these photos were in your victim's box containing his military stuff. They appear to be pictures of various groups of men and women whom he served with at different times in his career from boot camp to his last assignment."

"What did he do in the military?" Jill asked.

"He worked in an area called *machine operator and repair*. More than that vague description, I don't know. When I looked it up, it sounded like a common title that is used on almost every base. So he has about six group photos with different members of the military. Since they are all wearing uniforms, I can't tell them apart and even if I could, there are no names for us to research. I suggest you lend me your laptop so I can use Henrik's facial-recognition software to identify them, then I'll pass them on to the rest of you to investigate," Angela said.

Jill nodded. "Sounds like a plan. I'll use my phone while you have my laptop."

A short time later, Angela wrote fifteen names on a space on the murder board. Then she resumed her identity search. Madison and Jill worked on the names and were shortly joined by Marie. Two hours later, when Jo arrived in the living room, the list had swelled to one hundred people and then was reduced as names were knocked off because they died or something in their background didn't match time-wise to the letters or Mr. Thomas's death.

A short time later, the murder board was down to twenty names. That was still a lot of names, and they had no idea if any of them was the actual murderer, but at least they had a start. In the last twenty-four hours, Jill's team had narrowed their focus thanks to the letter on the victim's phone and the pictures he'd kept from his military service.

By the end of the day, they were closer to understanding who and why. They had the list down to three men whom Ed had served with. They had also narrowed their research to a couple of different groups that were proposing insurrections of the government. Getting into the chat rooms and reading the posts of these groups depressed everyone who read the posts. They were full of conspiracy theories and what seemed to Jill and her team as illogical conclusions.

"I feel slimy after reading all of these chat room comments from groups that want to overthrow the government. Let's go out to dinner somewhere and forget about these people," Marie suggested.

"Yeah, I agree," Jill said. "These chat rooms are so filled with bullshit that after a while you want to shower. What kind of restaurant are you thinking of?" Jill asked, thinking about the variety in the nation's capital.

"This might sound like a weird idea, but we could get sandwiches and go sit on the National Mall near the Lincoln Memorial and try to remember what we like about our government. I mean, it isn't by any means perfect, but there are many worse places in the world, and especially for women."

"That's not a bad idea," Jo said. "The weather is nice for fall. Are there any chairs we could take with us stored in this condo?"

In short order, they found a sandwich shop, lightweight folding chairs, and locations where they would be allowed to set up a picnic dinner on the National Mall. An hour after the suggestion, they were settled in a small circle with sandwiches and sodas. It was a great place to watch people and catch up on each other's lives. While they stayed in contact frequently, they hadn't seen each other since Jill and Nathan's wedding.

"Marie, I'm sorry I pulled you away from Henrik's visit. Did you have plans to at least dine together while he was in the state?" Jill said.

"No. He had meetings and dinners scheduled in Milwaukee and Chicago. I had meetings in Green Bay that I couldn't reschedule, so the only time we spent together was on the phone. It's okay. He's passionate about his company, and so I'd rather vacation later when we have each other's full attention, than in the middle of important business transactions."

Jill thought about saying something else and instead decided to change the subject. "Madison, what are your thoughts about this case and a future in private investigations?"

"Consider me your sponge. I'm soaking up every moment of this investigation, what everyone is doing, how you go about investigating, and especially how you've woven in the skills of your friends. I think that if you're going to do a stressful and complicated job like this one, then you ought to have your friends along for the ride."

Jill's friends seated in a circle smiled at her intern. Then Jill added, "My friends don't like the job when someone is after us. I thought I was going to lose Nathan and Jo to the violence of this job, but they both stuck with me."

Jo looked up and said, "I'll admit I'm easily scared and we have been chased by all kinds of criminals, but it is also really good when we get the criminals in the end."

As one, they looked up as they heard shouts nearby and tried to locate the source of the commotion. They flung themselves flat on the grass when they heard what sounded like gunshots to their inexperienced ears. Then people began running around them. On the heels of that were police sirens. Jill listened again to the sounds and the hysteria of the people moving past them. There was no mention of wounds, blood, or anyone being hit. What was going on?

There was noise of police activity from perhaps a football field length away. Jill decided to stand up and take cover behind a tree and see if she could determine what was going on. Using her phone camera to zoom in on the bright lights and activity up ahead, she nodded to her friends who had been watching her from the ground.

"I think it's safe to stand up. I think that might have been a recording."

"Seriously? I hope the police arrest those idiots. Someone could have been hurt running away from the sound," Marie said, standing up and peering toward where Jill was looking.

Jill had an idea and said, "I'm going to move closer."

Madison followed while her three friends stayed with their picnic supplies and started to clean up. They had a feeling they wouldn't finish the picnic tonight.

"What did you see?" Madison asked, trailing Jill. She wondered what her mentor was up to and could only assume that she was safe.

"That might have been a militia group causing the panic."

Militia group? Madison pondered and then she understood. "You're wondering if that's our insurrectionist group."

Jill nodded.

$\mathcal{J}$ill had crept closer, hoping to hear the conversation between law enforcement and the group of men who seemed to be at the heart of the commotion. She was focused on listening, but recognized that her entire team was close by listening as well.

"Can we add a complaint to the police about this group using a bad recording? We don't know if anyone was injured running away from this area." Jo asked.

"Yes we can, but I think the police have the evidence in front of them. Let's move closer and stick our noses where they don't belong," Jill said, closing the gap between where she stood and where the group of police officers in riot gear had men in camo outfits surrounded. The men were being forced to the ground, while guns were held on them.

Jill looked around to see her team wasn't the only spectators watching. Other pedestrians in the area had their cameras out and were filming the crowd. Jill caught Angela's eye and she winked back at her. Message sent and received. Angela would have numerous photos of the suspects and bystanders. Jill tried to hear who was saying what. The law-enforcement folks were backing up spectators away from the scene. One of the men on the ground was speaking in a loud voice about his constitutional rights. Meanwhile, one of the officers was examining the boom box and recordings that this group of men had. Jill decided to try and insert herself into the problem.

"Officer, I was seated over there," Jill said, pointing to the clearing where they had been enjoying their picnic. "We were enjoying a nice picnic dinner when all of a sudden we heard what sounded like gunshot sounds. We hit the ground as many people in this area started to run away. I hope no one got hurt."

"Ma'am, if you'll wait over there, we'll take your statement in a few minutes," the officer said, pointing to an area near the boom box. He obviously wanted to get her out of hearing range of their suspects before taking her statement. She moved as directed and observed her teammates doing an awesome job taking photographs or listening to conversations.

Jill waited patiently and watched as the men were taken to what might be called a paddy wagon and were secured inside. After the doors closed and the vehicle left, an officer returned to her and a few other spectators.

"Hi, I'm Officer Jerome Brown, and I'd like to take your statement. For the record, please state your name and address."

Jill did so.

"What were you doing in this area tonight and what did you hear?"

Jill debated how much to tell the officer and decided to give him the full story. After hearing that explanation, the officer was giving her the squint eye.

"So Dr. Quint, you just happen to be picnicking near where a group of men unhappy with the government decided to stage an event?"

"Yes."

"If you are who you say you are, you know we don't like coincidences."

"Yes, imagine my surprise at having such a clue dropped in my lap. Of course, that was only after I realized that we were listening to a recording and not real gunshots. Still, I had flattened myself on the grass and watched many tourists hurry away, so I wasn't the only one who thought they were hearing gunshots."

"What was the name again of the detective you say you're working with on this case?"

"Detective Chambers. His office is in the large rectangular police building near here."

"Please stand here for a minute."

The officer left Jill in place and stepped away to make a phone call, keeping an eye on her. About five minutes later he returned.

"Just when you think you've seen and heard everything on the job, something new, like you Dr. Quint, pops up. I did verify your identity with the detective and he is on his way here. He also has an interest in the group we arrested this evening. He asked that you remain here."

"Of course. I'll gather up my team and we'll continue our picnic over there until you're ready to chat with us."

"Okay, please don't talk about what you heard or saw as we may wish to interview other members of your team."

"Of course."

Jill waved at her friends and they soon settled back on the chairs munching sandwiches again.

"Can I just say that if this is what the life of a private detective looks like, I can't wait to start my own firm."

The women all smiled at the young protege.

"I'd say something, but we've been warned not to talk," Jill said, smiling. "But after the police are done with us, I'm sure we'll all have something to tell you, Madison. Shall we talk about football? I don't think that will get us in trouble."

Fifteen minutes later they had deeply analyzed the Green Bay Packers and their football season, which was at about the midpoint. Officer Brown and Detective Chambers approached the group having heard the last of their discussion.

"Ladies, thank you for not talking about what you heard tonight. From the little bit that I heard of your conversation, ESPN should be calling you with analyst jobs at any moment," Brown said. "I won't ask you about our local team—the Commanders—as we seem headed for another mediocre season."

"I already interviewed Dr. Quint on what she heard. We have enough local witnesses that we don't need your witness statements, so you may all talk about what you heard and saw tonight. Detective, they are all yours."

"Jill, you didn't mention that you were bringing an entire team here to help with the case. What happened?" asked Detective Chambers.

Jill introduced the team and their function. "It was finding that first letter that specifically named insurrectionists that unnerved me. A single killer that you're after presents a certain level of danger. When you're up against a group of crazy radicals, that's a whole other level of danger. Seeing the crazies in this park tonight verified that I made the right decision to see if I could get help today. We have pictures of the men and the crowd and we'll do facial-recognition searches on everyone to see if they are involved in the Ed Thomas case."

"You think it will be that easy?"

"No, but there is a certain level of similarity in the dumbness of the criminals in each case.

In the first case, they wanted Ed Thomas to print a new currency for their insurrectionist group. That's all fine, but who would cash that currency? They weren't thinking. Similarly tonight, a group of men wanted to announce their group's platform and chose introductory music featuring recordings of gunshots, which was sure to bring the police down on them before they had the chance to discuss much of their platform."

"True. From what the officer described, these men didn't see the harmful effects to the public from hearing the recorded sounds of automatic weapons. They were totally surprised to learn that someone had sprained their ankle hurrying away from them. They didn't want people running away; they were using the sounds to show how powerful they were. My impression was the elevator didn't run to the top of these insurrectionist brains."

"Exactly. Maybe when you join one of these groups, you have to suspend your common sense and thinking ability and just go with the flow because you agree with the mission. On the other hand, I'm hoping we lucked out and this is the shadow group behind Ed Thomas's murder."

"We never have that kind of luck in our cases, so I doubt it, but I'll let you know."

Jill nodded and turned to walk away, which made the detective suspicious. In his experience, she usually stuck her nose in police business.

"Wait a minute," the detective said. "You're up to something. Tell me what you plan to do."

Jill smiled and gave kudos to the detective. "My team filmed the men your department arrested. We should have them identified later tonight and know if any of them served in the military with Ed Thomas. We have photos from his military days and we'll try to make a connection if there is one."

"I wish I had the time to look over your shoulder while you investigate this lot, but as you know, I have work waiting for me back at the office. Call me if you find any connection."

"Of course. Will you be releasing any of these men tonight?"

"Probably not, but if your group finds anything on them or if we do when we run their identities through the system, that will extend their stay with us."

Jill nodded and turned to join her friends as they picked up their picnic and prepared to return to the condominium.

When they got back to their computers, Angela located the best pictures of the insurrectionists and sent them to Jill for her to put through the facial-recognition software. They quickly had an identification of most of the men. They had various prior criminal and civil charges in their backgrounds. Some had military service as well, but the years were wrong to have served with Ed Thomas. The men who belonged to the group tonight were too young to have served alongside their victim. She dropped an email to the detective summarizing the men arrested that night, along with their records and the fact that they were too young to have served with Ed Thomas.

Darn, Jill thought. She hoped they would have new leads from their interrupted dinner, but it looked like that was out of the question. Eventually they called it quits for the night. Jill did her usual call with Nathan and then mentally reviewed the clues they had before falling asleep. She was aware that she would be losing her friends' help in about thirty-six hours and she felt the pressure to make progress on the case.

Once again, Jill was up first the next morning, followed by Madison. "Did you find anything new last night after I went to bed?"

"We did. I think we might have limited the letter writer to three people, so that's a big step forward. Angela found people based on the pictures in our victim's belongings, then Marie went to work."

"Wow, that is great news. Certainly if we can find an individual, we may be able to find the insurrectionist group behind him," Jill said, looking up at her murder board to see if her teammates had added any names or information she could follow up with that morning. She smiled when she saw three new names in Marie's handwriting—there it was, a clue as to the killer.

She opened her laptop and went to work on the three names. They were all males, so Jill took a little side trip investigating whether she should look for female suspects. After diving down a rabbit hole into female participation in militias worldwide, she decided to park that information in the back of her brain. The insurrectionist group might contain females; the fake delivery person who picked up Ed Thomas's Chinese food might even have been a female. The three people in the pictures that her team thought might be involved in this case were all males. Once they woke up, she would have to make sure that they didn't exclude females as a matter of routine, but given that they had dealt with female killers in the past, she doubted that the team had automatically excluded them.

Marie had sketched a light dossier of each name. She had ran out of time to do anything in depth. So Jill took it from there. She agreed with Angela's and Marie's assessment that these three individuals should be added to the suspect list.

Jill thought of another question and asked Madison, "Did Jo research the funding of these insurrectionists?"

"She did. She said it is depressing to study, but it doesn't contribute to our quest to find the murderer. That's a quote from her."

"Thanks. I didn't think that information would help us pinpoint our insurrectionist group. Still, I needed to look into it."

By noon they had identified and researched anyone remotely connected to their victim and still the same three names remained on the murder board.

Jill owed Melanie an update and was about to call her when her cell phone rang with Melanie's caller ID.

"Hi Melanie, I was just about to call you. I have a brief update."

"I need you to come over to my apartment. I just received my first threatening letter and it sounds like it's from the same author as my father's letters."

"We're on our way," she said and they ended the call.

"Let's take a ride over to Melanie's apartment. She's received a letter similar to the ones her father received," Jill said to her friends. A short time later the five women were in a car heading to Melanie's address. They hadn't been there before, but the GPS got them there accurately.

Jill performed introductions between Melanie and Marie, Jo,

and Angela. Then they all read the letter that Melanie had received.

"I agree that your letter sounds like the same author. Where did you find the letter?" Angela said.

"It was sticking out of a delivery box on my front step."

"Do you have a camera focused on that area?" Marie asked.

"No."

"Do you think your apartment has been searched?" Jill asked.

Melanie looked terrified by that thought, then looked around her apartment and ended with, "No."

"Given the events at your father's house and the start of letters being sent to you, I think you should expect that. I would add some security to your home," Jill said. "What is also interesting is the mention of plates in this letter. I don't think we're talking about dinner plates. I suspect this refers to the plates used in producing currency."

Melanie frowned, thinking about conversations she'd had with her father. Had he ever mentioned plates? "Dad might have mentioned plates in one of our conversations. I think he'd had an easy day at work as the press was down while they replaced the plates used to make the various currencies. Without that, there was nothing for his cutting machine to do, so their supervisor had them catch up on mandatory safety training and other education while the plates were being installed, or something like that."

"Was there a mention of plates in the first letter your father received?" Angela asked.

"I don't think so," Jill said, pulling up a copy of the letter on her phone and reading. "However, this letter refers to an in-person conversation and maybe the plates were mentioned then. So if you get the plates, and I presume they are for sheets of currency rather than individual bills, then you still need the right paper and ink, and you need to cut the bills with precision."

"Yes, but I thought in an earlier conversation that the insurrectionists wanted to print their own currency. Why would they need a plate for that?" Jo asked.

"Good question. Maybe these guys aren't as dumb as we thought. They want to print their own currency—not a new currency, but rather a counterfeit currency. That's an old-school approach to funding your passion," Marie suggested.

"Do any of our suspects have a background in printing? I wouldn't think you could take just anyone off the street and have them print money. Someone would have to know about paper and ink and cutting," Madison said.

"True," Jo and Marie said simultaneously.

"So do they think that Ed Thomas somehow walked out of the mint holding a large sheet of metal and no one noticed? Furthermore, do these insurrectionists think that Ed gave it to his daughter?" Jill said, trying to follow the logic of the story.

Everyone was silent while they pondered what was going on.

Just then Jill's phone rang and she saw that it was Detective Chambers calling. She held up her hand to the group and said, "It's the detective."

"We interviewed the guys today that we arrested last evening.One guy in particular had some information about another insurrectionist group. I think he might have knowledge of the group that sent letters to our victim and Thomas."

"Did he give you the name of the group?" Jill asked.

"He did, and we've been trying to research the group in our detectives division. However, your team might do better with the research. The name of the group is 7%."

"Are you sure? Isn't there a right-wing group called the Three Percenters? What's the likelihood of the two groups having similar names?"

"I wondered about that too, and we questioned him several times to make sure that he believed the name of the group was 7%."

"We've been unable to find any information about the group.

We're not sure it exists. That's why I'm calling you. If your crack team can't find the group, then we'll consider our suspect to have made up the name."

Marie and Jo went to work trying to locate the company. Marie found it first. "It's registered in French. It's Les Sept Pour Cent. It originated in France, spread to Canada, and then to the United States. Their idea is that no more than 7 percent taxation should pay for government."

"Damn, your team is good," Detective Chambers said. "Can you text me that name so I have the spelling right?"

Jill handed her phone to Marie to type in the name of the group, and she hit send.

"It should be there now," Jill said as they all heard a ping come through the speaker phone. "What does 7% want with currency plates? I'm not making the connection."

"That makes two of us," said the detective. "I'm going to hang up now so we can research this group."

"Detective, you know we're not your personal wikipedia. Call me when you need help, not as a last resort."

"I will. You must know that we cops don't like working with civilians. I'll adjust my attitude, but I may fall into old habits."

It was the closest thing to an apology that she'd ever received from a cop. Usually, they let her into their cases planning on her being a target for the bad guys. So this partial apology and acceptance felt huge.

They ended their call and Jill and her team wrapped up their time at Melanie's apartment. They got into the car and once they returned to their apartment Jill asked Marie and Jo to research the group while she, Angela, and Madison went to another area of the apartment to try to reason why this insurrectionist group might have caused Ed Thomas's death and why they would want currency plates from the government.

CHAPTER 10

"*L*et's brainstorm, no matter how wild an idea that could connect this group to our victim."

"Just because you believe that 7 percent is the right level of taxation, that doesn't mean that you wouldn't want your own confederate cash to power your group's mission. To have the idea approved, it would take changes in the government, but this group doesn't seem the patient type to wait for that process to occur." Jill started with an idea.

"How about there's actually another group behind this one and they are influencing this group to do stupid stuff for their own reasons?" Angela suggested.

Jill looked at Madison for her first suggestion and she was like a deer in the headlights.

Jill prompted, "Think of a wild idea; don't tell yourself that your idea is not worthy."

"Okay, how about if this group has no plan to overturn the government; rather, the leaders are collecting dues from the men in a Ponzi-type scheme."

Jill and Angela smiled at their mentee coming up with her wild idea. They reached over and high-fived her. Then they went back to ideas.

"Okay, how about the French originators of this idea gave up in France and came to America to see if they could get people on board? Someone in the French Army served alongside Ed and asked him to print money for their effort," Angela suggested.

They continued down the track on stranger and stranger ideas, and looked up when Jo and Marie approached.

"We think this is a giant fake-conspiracy group intending to raise money. They have no intention of trying to overthrow the government; they just want to try and get rich by having the other men carry out actions that will pour money into their coffers," Marie said.

"I looked at the finances of this group and they have a few 'executives' paid outrageous salaries," Jo said.

"So what's the connection to our victim?" Jill asked.

"We don't know. We don't know if they were recruiting him to be a part of their group and thought he could really boost their earnings. Or were the executives behind this really wanting the currency plates and developed this elaborate scheme to get them?" Marie said.

"What's going on with the French group?" Angela asked. "Is it active?"

"It has sort of faded into oblivion and I haven't made a connection between the French group and our group other than their name. The French group doesn't have any funding at the moment and never did have much," Jo said.

"But these executives could be filling these guys' heads with stories of glory, and they're too lazy or don't know how to check the validity of those claims. It wouldn't be the first time that a cult-like group of followers didn't fact-check the validity of their claims," Marie said.

"I think we brainstormed some wild ideas for the connection between Ed and the 7 Percenters. Now we need to add Melanie.

She doesn't work at the Bureau of Printing and Engraving, so why go after her? Why would they think that Melanie would have any connection to their scheme?" Jill asked.

"Maybe it's like your other cases that you told me about. Maybe they are after her to see what she knows about the investigation and more importantly, what evidence we're coming up with. If Security at the Bureau of Printing and Engraving is in on the scheme, then they know of Melanie's relationship to her father. Perhaps they researched who you were from the visitor logs when you went there yesterday?" Madison suggested.

"That's a good idea. I like that suggestion," Jill said. "So should we expect to be attacked here or have our premises searched? How would they know where we're staying?"

"Perhaps someone followed us back here from Melanie's house. We weren't looking and anyone could have followed us, and I wouldn't notice it unless they tailgated me or I saw them weaving in traffic. Since this apartment is a loaner, let's hope they leave us alone here," Madison said.

"Yes. Fortunately we have more security on this place than Melanie had on hers, so we'll have some warning if anyone tries to invade our temporary home," Jill said.

"So where are we, and what are our next steps?" Angela asked.

"Good question. We really need to brainstorm with the detective's people. I'll call him as I forgot to tell him about the search of Melanie's apartment. Then I'll suggest we meet to discuss what we've found. Let's see if he still has respect for us."

She contacted the detective and made her pitch. "Detective, when you called earlier I was at Melanie's apartment. She had a letter delivered to her similar to her father's and it was tucked into a package on her doorstep. The package was an internet purchase and had nothing to do with the letter—it was simply tucked inside—but the style and tone were similar to the letters her father received," Jill said, planning to continue when the detective cut her off.

"How could you forget to tell me that?"

"Because our entire conversation quickly morphed into a discussion about the 7% group. I simply forgot. Now, my team has a lot more information about the group and we want to meet with your team to brainstorm. We can reason out the connection between them and Melanie."

"Just a moment," the detective said as he put the call on hold.

"Hmmm, I don't know if he put me on hold to swear and pull his hair out, or if he's thinking of inviting us in."

"I don't recall him having any hair last night," Angela said.

"True. I guess that means he's going to invite us into the inner sanctum," Jo said optimistically.

Jill held up her fingers showing that they were crossed.

After what felt like a lifetime, the phone line reconnected and the detective said, "Can you be here in thirty minutes?"

"Sure. See you soon," Jill said and the call ended. She high-fived each of her friends individually. "Let's bring all of our stuff to the meeting, and blow these detectives out of the water with our research and ideas."

Her team smiled at her enthusiasm, and knew how the game was played.

Right on schedule, they were shown into a conference room with three bored detectives in addition to Detective Chambers. Jill debated about whether to take the men head-on or let it slide. She decided to let it slide until that went too far. Introductions were made and then the detective asked Jill to discuss what they had found regarding the 7% group. At the end of Jo's and Marie's discussion, the detectives looked a little less sour faced about the contributions of the civilians. They had provided them with new information. Once they exhausted their questions about the group, Jill decided it was her turn.

"So my team has speculated about what is going on. Why would they target the victim's daughter? She has nothing to do with the Bureau of Printing and Engraving. Here are some of our theories." Jill proceeded to lay out the ideas they had brainstormed. Then she asked the detectives for theirs.

"This is an ongoing investigation and we can't reveal any of our evidence," said one of the detectives.

"So this entire invite was just a hoax. You want all the information we've collected but you're unwilling to discuss motives? Theories about the players involved in the case is not evidence. Do you have any theories?" Jill realized she had lost her patience with the group of detectives. It was one step forward, two steps backward.

"Actually, my men are not saying anything because we did have the information about the daughter's letter. Let's discuss our ideas now," said the detective, trying to ease the tension between the two groups.

"Before we dive into that, given everything you know at the moment about this case, do you think Melanie Thomas is safe to stay in her apartment?" Angela asked.

"I think she is probably personally safe, but perhaps her apartment is not. Do you have room for her in the place you're staying at the moment?" replied Detective Chambers.

"We do. I'll text her right now about moving there later today," Jill said.

"So these men who are after her think that she has something related to her father's job making currency. It seems like there's a rumor that he somehow got a plate from the Bureau of Printing and Engraving," said one of the detectives.

"Have you seen those plates that the mint uses? They are not-single currency plates; rather, they are used to print the whole page. There are four rows of eight notes for a total of thirty-two bills on each plate. So I think the plates are at least three feet by three feet. Even if you tucked such an item under a parka and walked out, Security searches you."

"I wonder why they think he has the plate and now his daughter possesses it."

"Perhaps they think he got one out of the mint to fund her company, which is not true. He took a loan out against his retirement plan and she's on track to pay him back in three years. That is something most parents would do," Jo said.

Jill smiled to herself when she noted the detectives writing things down. Her team was really good and she was proud of how they all helped solve cases.

"Perhaps there's a missing plate from the Bureau and someone blamed him or started a rumor it was Ed. Remember, the security guys were no help with the threatening letters he received," Marie said.

"Yes, they were certainly obstructing us today. How would we find out if a plate is missing from the Bureau?" Jill asked.

Detective Chambers grabbed his head as though that was a question too far. "He died on federal property and now we're asking about a missing item from federal property. I'm going to have to get my lieutenant involved so we can speak to someone in the Treasury Department. If something weird is going on in the Bureau of Printing and Engraving, they'll want to know."

"I thought you had access to this case as a murder investigation is outside of their expertise and the murder weapon was from a Chinese restaurant in your district and his body was stolen. His daughter is going to be next if someone truly believes she is sitting on a currency plate of one-hundred dollar bills," Jill said.

"Just a moment," the Detective said as he got up and left the conference room. They were left with the unfriendly detectives.

"Where did you get your financial information from?" one of them asked. "We didn't even think to look at the information you looked at."

It was a nice concession from the detectives and Jo showed the detective where she looked up the information. It was a start, and Jill hoped they could build on that.

CHAPTER 11

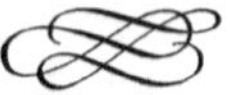

*D*etective Chambers was gone for half an hour. The time was so long that they began to wonder if he was coming back, and then the door opened.

"Okay, the Lieu is putting a call in to a contact in the Treasury Department and we'll see if we can get anywhere going around the Bureau."

"When will you have an answer?"

"I'm hoping today, and if the planets align, in the next hour."

"Okay, then have you gentlemen told us everything you know about this case? Did anything special come out of the locker—any pictures? We've gone through his military pictures and identified three suspects. Do you have any suspects on your list?" Jill asked.

"What do you mean, you've identified three suspects? How?" asked another detective who had been quiet up to that point.

"The threatening letters to Mr. Thomas refer to a friendship from his years of military service. We took the pictures of his time in the military which he kept in a separate box. We used facial recognition to identify his friends or company at the time he served. Then we looked into their backgrounds and were able to eliminate all of them except for three."

"Wow. If your guesses are correct, then you're further along than we are here. Give us the names and why you've identified them as a suspect," Chambers said.

Jill wrote on the dry-erase board, while Marie explained their backgrounds.

"I don't think I've given you the respect you deserve. My apologies," said Chambers at the end of Marie's explanation.

"Why don't we locate these three suspects and interview them while we're waiting for action from the higher-ups," Chambers said as his detectives went to work finding a location for the men.

"Good idea. Are we finished talking about motives here?" Jill asked. "We gave you ours, but do you have any other ideas that we can research? Not to brag, but we're really good at research."

She heard nothing but silence, so she added, "Let's catalog what we don't know. Here's my list: is there a missing plate at the Bureau, what's the connection of this group to Melanie, what is the purpose of the 7% beyond making three executives rich, have you looked at every road camera to see if you can identify the food delivery person, is the end game strictly about making counterfeit money, what is going on with the Treasury security folks— do they belong to the 7%? What are your thoughts, detectives?" Two of the detectives had left to find the physical locations of the three men on Jill's suspect list. They were left with Chambers and one other detective.

"I don't know if we have enough information to examine a motive yet," Chambers said as the other detective tried to be inscrutable.

"Sometimes identifying the motive helps you find the murderer," Jill said. She looked at her watch and added, "My team departs for Wisconsin in three hours. I think we'll return to our apartment and research the security personnel at the Bureau. Maybe that will help us figure out some of the picture behind this murder and the letter-writing."

Jill and her friends stood up to leave. Detective Chambers

opened his mouth to say something, but then nothing came out. It was her impression that he wanted her and her team to stay so he and his fellow detectives could learn more, and yet he detested the fact that she had explored avenues he hadn't thought of yet. In the end, he asked if they needed an escort out of the building, to which Jill shook her head.

On the way out, Jill checked her email to see if Melanie had responded. She had, and she was ready to move but was waiting for Jill's notification of when they would be back at their lodging. They let her know they were on the way and would meet her there soon.

"What's your impression of the detectives?" Jo asked.

"We had them on our side for a while, and then they went back into their true form of 'we're trained detectives' and 'we're better than you.' It's a shame, but not surprising," Jill said. "They must have a course in that way of thinking at the police academy. Oh well, I do think our time is better served by returning to the condo and investigating the security force of the Bureau."

"Henrik's pilot noted that on our return to the airport, we'll enter a private gate and be onboard quickly. We don't have to think about getting to the airport at least an hour in advance," Marie said.

"I'll drop you guys off; just give me a time we should leave," Jill said, wanting to spend all the time possible with her friends. The buzzer to their apartment rang, and they found that Melanie had arrived.

Jill showed her to a room and told her the plans for the evening. Melanie and Madison would stay behind while Jill dropped her friends off at the airport.

Marie went to work on identifying the names of people employed by the security services at the Bureau. In no time, she had perhaps one hundred names of employees.

"How do you do that?" Madison asked.

"Social media is so pervasive. Even if your employer orders

you to stay off of it, people can get caught in other people's photos and videos. What would be really helpful would be to have our friend Henrik hack into the DC camera system and get pictures of employees as they are leaving the Bureau of Printing and Engraving, but I don't think I'll ask him as he's super busy at the convention and then he's off somewhere else."

"We can't use him in every investigation despite his usefulness. Madison, that's something to look for when you're assembling your team—you need a computer expert and, better still, someone with hacking skills. That activity is illegal, but there's an entire group of hackers who would savor helping with an investigation. It's illegal per the law, but noble in their minds. Just don't tell me or anyone else about your hacker and think of some far-fetched excuses for information that a hacker obtained for you," Jill advised. "Marie, can you knock off about 90 percent of the list before you leave? I'd love to also have Jo's evaluation of any suspects for their financial transactions. There has to be something shady there."

There was silence in the room except for the keyboard clattering until shortly before they needed to head to the airport. Marie and Jo provided summaries of their findings and they were off to drive to the airport. About halfway there, she noticed headlights in her rear-view mirror that seemed to have been there a while. There was a private entrance to the airfield and the car drove past. Jill debated saying anything and decided not to worry her friends. She would ask if there was another exit to this airport once her friends were dropped off.

With hugs and final bits of advice, Jill watched as the door closed on the sleek private jet and walked through the tiny terminal looking for someone to ask about exits. She spotted an employee and approached them.

"Hi, I just dropped some friends off here and need to return home. However, I think someone might have followed me here. Is there another exit from the airfield?"

"Would you like me to call the police?"

"No. It's dark out and maybe I was wrong about the headlamps following me. Do you have a service entrance or something?"

"We do. We're not supposed to let people out that way, but given your concern, I'll call Security and have them escort you out that gate."

"Thank you. I really appreciate it. I don't know if my feeling was made up from my imagination, or if someone was indeed following me."

Jill tried to look shaky about her experience to the employee to get more help and sympathy. She wasn't really worried about coming to harm. She could fight most of her own battles, but there was no reason to make it easy for someone to do harm to her. She waited for about fifteen minutes for Security to show up and then followed their car to a different area of the airfield to exit. Thank goodness for GPS as she was in a foreign city and didn't know her way back to the apartment, but the talking voice was directing her to her temporary home. After she left the airfield and saw no one following behind her, she hit the on-ramp for the freeway and called Nathan just to chat. Seeing her friends leave was always a downer and he would cheer her up.

"Hey Sweetie," Jill said.

"Hello, what are you up to? Did your friends just leave?" Nathan knew when Angela, Marie, and Jo had to leave and did the calculation.

"They did, and I'm sad and I know you'll cheer me up."

"I'll send you Trixie and Arthur videos and that will make you laugh, but I sense you're driving. When you get back to your apartment, you can laugh. Have you found your murderer? Do the police respect you?"

Jill chuckled. "You always know my pain points. I think I was followed to the airfield, so I had Security's assistance in exiting through a service entrance and I haven't noticed the headlights in my rear-view mirror. So you'll keep me calm on the drive back to the apartment. I'm talking to you looking out the windshield and getting eyeball whiplash, bouncing between the windshield and the rear-view mirror. But all is quiet there."

"Are you in danger?" Nathan asked with concern in his voice. Over the years of their relationship, Jill had been targeted by an international sniper, a crazed skier, and a couple of crazed drivers; and someone had even tried to throw her over a castle wall. He had reason to be concerned.

"I'm good at the moment. This is a strange case. We've been here a few days researching this case, and all we have so far is speculative motives and speculative suspects. I don't get the letter writing. I don't understand the currency plates and their role in any of this. All I really know is that Ed Thomas was murdered."

"Wow, you usually know more by now—and that's even with the help of your team. Do you have an end date for this case?"

"Sort of. My client said she could fund us for a week and we're three days into that week. In theory, I'll be flying home no later than four days from now."

"In theory."

"Yeah, you know me. I won't be able to walk away from this mystery. My victim deserves justice, and he doesn't have it yet."

They chatted a little more about each other's lives. Jill hadn't noticed anyone following her and she turned onto the street, which had a gate arm into a private parking garage. It was a vulnerable period of time when she had the window down and was waiting for the gate arm to open. Worst of all, it was dark. Sure, there was lighting around the building, but there were many shadows that someone could hide in. She decided to go around the block a second time and asked Madison to come out with her cell phone in case of trouble. Maybe she was paranoid, but better paranoid than dead.

On her second turn around the block, she met Madison at the gate arm. The garage door opened and she guided the car in slowly as Madison walked behind her. Madison walked with her back to Jill's car, holding a bright flashlight to illuminate the driveway. Jill laughed at her overkill, but this was a strange case, and it paid to be safe. She parked the car and Madison waited at the trunk.

"I didn't see anyone out there, did you?"

"No, but I could swear the same set of headlights followed me all the way to the airfield. I contacted airport Security and exited through a service exit on the other side of the airfield. So whoever was following me may have been hoping to follow me back here, but they missed me. I was talking to Nathan on the way here and said this is one of our stranger cases, and that we don't have any strong suspects, nor do we understand the motive yet."

"Yeah, it seemed like you solved the case much faster in Asheville. Granted, someone tried to burn me up in a house fire. I'll take a slower-solved case if my home doesn't have to catch on fire."

Jill smiled at her intern, "That's a positive way of looking at it. How is Melanie doing?"

"She's rather overwhelmed. She's planning her father's funeral and she's getting these goofy letters and we're not making any progress even though clearly the case is progressing. I'm glad you had her move over to our apartment. Our company is making her feel safer, and I think she feels good about hiring you when she was watching your team work on the case. Everyone was serious; everyone had their own skill set. So I think it's going as well as it could."

"Thanks for that feedback. I'm frustrated at the speed of this case, too. You should not expect to solve things in a week. But you want to for many reasons. You want to do it for your client. You know that your client doesn't have an unlimited budget to support your detective work. It's also hard on your ego dealing with law enforcement as they never take us seriously, no matter how many cases we've solved. Oh well, this is turning out to be a great training session for you. Let's get back inside and continue our work."

When Jill and Madison walked into the apartment's living room, Melanie was staring at her phone with a paralyzed look on her face.

"Melanie, what's wrong?" Jill asked.

"I just got a threatening text message on my phone. The message says I should fire your team and send you back to wherever you came from."

"Let me read it—Madison, take a picture of it while I'm reading it in case it disappears."

Jill looked over Melanie's shoulder and read the message as she scrolled through it. The tone of it was much like the written letters. Melanie was ordered to fire Jill's team or else, but the writer never said what the actual threat was. That was strange.

"Can you forward that message to me?" Jill asked.

Melanie did so and Jill saved it before sending it on to the detective. Then she called him. It was after his normal working hours, but he could let her call go to voicemail if he didn't want to talk to her.

"Detective Chambers."

"Hi, Detective, it's Jill. I forwarded you a threatening message that Melanie received on her phone. My team has identified most of the security staff and researched them. Did our initial three suspects prove fruitful?"

She heard the detective sigh, probably because he was processing the different pieces of information she had just relayed. She wondered what his first question would be. She made an internal bet that it would be about the security staff.

"Okay, I just read the message that Ms. Thomas received. The tone is like the written letters, but it's strange that the threat is not described. It's more of an eight-year-old kid on a playground saying you better not do that, or else."

Whoops, she lost the bet with herself. She replied, "Yeah, I thought that was kind of strange too that the message didn't have an explicit threat. What about the suspects? Did your detectives find them?

"They did not. They were not at their homes, nor at their work locations. We did get a match with one of the faces to the vehicle that abducted Mr. Thomas's remains."

"That's good news. Were you able to secure a warrant for his arrest?"

"Yes."

"But the other two men that I put on my suspect list were not in the fake mortuary van?" Jill asked, thinking it was like pulling teeth to get the detective to spill any details.

"We don't know one way or the other, as there wasn't a clear picture of the other people in the van."

Did you find the van?"

"No. It's a little more difficult as it's likely out of the District and in Virginia somewhere."

"Am I cutting into your family time, Detective? If so, I can meet you at your office tomorrow with details about the people who work in the Security department at the Bureau of Printing and Engraving."

"There never really is off duty for a detective unless you leave the state on vacation. Tell me what you have about the security force."

"As you may have guessed, there are over one hundred employees in that division. Given all the money they need to guard, that's not surprising. My financial expert was able to target about fifteen of them for suspicious transactions. I'll send you that information. Have you heard back from your lieutenant as to whether he's made progress with his contact in the Treasury Department?"

"He was having dinner with his contact and they're likely still at it. Let me take a look at your financial information and I'll get it to the lieutenant in hopes that he can insert that into their conversation."

There was a switch sound, and then the email was sent.

"It should be in your inbox now. Call me when you have an update, please."

"Please stay on the line while I make sure I understand what I'm reading."

There was dead silence as the detective read the email and its attachments.

"This is pretty good stuff. I'm not a financial wizard, and yet I understand. The dollar transactions are very suspicious. Thank you for this information and let me get it over to my lieutenant now. Talk to you later."

The call ended and Jill massaged her head. She looked at her watch and decided it was time to call it quits for the day. There were activities that were happening that she had no role in but that might have an interesting result by morning.

She looked over at Melanie, who had a laptop in her lap and was probably working on her business and said, "I think we're done for the evening. I need law enforcement to move on a few things. I'm also brain dead, so I'll see you two in the morning."

"Thank you Jill, for all you've done so far. This is a much more complicated case than it was when I hired you a couple days ago. I like how you've been able to liaison with the police and light a fire under them. I'll see you in the morning."

Jill gave a little wave to Madison and disappeared down the hallway. Sometimes when she was working on a case, it was helpful to think in the dark about the various facts swirling around her. Unfortunately, tonight's thinking time in bed brought no new revelations as Jill drifted off to sleep.

CHAPTER 12

*J*ill awoke from a sound sleep as she thought she heard
sounds in the apartment. She lay in bed listening for
sounds and surveyed her available weapons. She took
the shade off the lamp and unplugged it while she listened for
sound. She crept to her bedroom door, lamp in hand, but texted
Madison and Melanie that someone was in the apartment.

She listened again, trying to determine how many people were
inside. Madison texted back asking what she should do.

Call 911

Done.

*Grab a lamp, remove the shade, and be ready to swing. Stand just
inside your door.*

Okay.

Jill's bedroom was the closest to the front door, so she thought
that her bedroom would likely be entered first. Another part of
her brain was wondering how whoever had entered their apartment had gotten by the security system. It sounded like the
intruder was getting closer. In her martial arts training, she
learned to slow her breath and focus. They had begun using
sticks, so in her case she would replace the stick with a lamp. She

planned to use an uppercut as that should hurt the intruder's face. She was posed.

The door opened slowly and someone stuck their head in to peer at the bed. Jill brought the lamp up sharply, catching the intruder's jaw. He fell backward in the hallway with a groan. One down, but was there more behind him? It was hard to hear over the man's groaning, but she heard no voices of a potential second intruder. Jill decided to stick her arm into the hallway and turn the light on. Their assailant was laying on the hallway floor groaning with his hands on his face. Madison opened her door a fraction and Jill waved her out. She listened for sirens, but didn't hear any.

"Let's tie him up. Use the lamp stand in your hand and hit him a second time if he tries to get up," Jill said as she raced into the kitchen for a roll of duct tape that she spied there. She no sooner arrived back at Madison's side when there was a knock on their apartment door and she heard the words, "Police, we're responding to a 911 call."

Jill looked through the peep hole and saw two officers in uniform, so she unlocked the door and invited them in.

"I hit the intruder in the face with a lamp and we were about to duct-tape him," Jill said, leading the officers to where the intruder lay on the hallway floor. Madison lowered the lamp and stepped back.

The officers got the man's name from his wallet, but he wouldn't say anything mostly because Jill might have broken his jaw in her attack with the lamp. In the end, they decided to send their suspect to the hospital before he would be booked into jail. The two officers took Jill's and Madison's statements. It seemed like an open-and-shut case as the intruder had used lock picks to break into the apartment. The alarm had gone off, but a prior occupant had turned the volume down. Before the police left with their suspect, Jill gained his name from the officers. It was unlikely they would know him as both women were from out of the area, but still the officer asked if they did.

Eventually, they went back to sleep and were drinking coffee when Melanie joined them in the morning.

"Thanks for moving me here. I got the first good night's rest since my father died."

Jill and Madison looked at each other and smiled.

"What?"

"We had an intruder last night whom the police hauled away to the hospital at about two in the morning," Jill said.

Melanie's face showed a variety of expressions as she was trying to assimilate Jill's sentence.

"Why the hospital?"

"I heard noise in the apartment, so I grabbed the lamp, took the shade off of it, and then swung it upward when the intruder entered my bedroom. I apparently pack quite a punch as I broke the man's jaw and neutralized him."

"Wow. I guess I should have you show me that move since it worked so well," she finally said after thinking about it.

"Some of my cases earlier in my career put my life in danger, so my boyfriend—and now husband—took me to a martial arts demonstration. He's a Master Black Belt in Hapkido. I choose TaiChi which is much more than the slow stretches you see seniors doing. It gives you the confidence to deal with something like an intruder. So I stood just inside my bedroom door, and when he stuck his head in, I swung the lamp base like I was hitting a homerun. I think that was what cracked his jaw."

Melanie looked at Madison and asked, "What's your martial art?"

"After this case is over and I return to Asheville, I'll begin researching the various martial arts studios and pick one. I like the fact that I don't need a knife or gun. This guy will probably have his jaw wired shut and be drinking liquids for a while. That will give him a lot of time to reflect on threatening women."

"Did he have a weapon on him?" Melanie asked.

"Fortunately, no. He did have lock picks. However, before both of you feel safe, just remember he doesn't need a knife or gun to strangle a woman," Jill said.

"Did he say why he was breaking in?" Melanie asked.

"He didn't say anything. He was too absorbed in his jaw pain. We'll have to wait to get answers out of him, but I've already directed Detective Chambers to him so we should get answers sooner rather than later. Once he has some pain meds, he can write out his answers to their questions," Jill said.

Melanie nodded, then said, "Wait, I thought this apartment was alarmed?"

"Yes, I wondered about that last night. I discovered the volume of the alarm was turned down. I've since fixed that. I hope we have a quiet night tonight. I'll be dragging at some point, having my sleep disrupted like that. Even after the cops left with the suspect, it's not like you can immediately fall back to sleep."

Jill's cell phone rang with two incoming calls at the same time. She'd never seen that before. She answered the call identified as belonging to Detective Chambers and texted Nathan that she would call him back.

"Hello, Detective."

"The next time you face an intruder, could you break his legs instead of his jaw, so we can get answers out of him?"

Jill chuckled at the request and said, "Sorry about that Detective. All I knew was there was an intruder in our apartment and I took a lamp base and swung for the fences, as they say in major league baseball. He was down and out and we were about to duck-tape him when the police arrived. So you haven't been able to interview him yet this morning?"

"No, they had to give him anesthesia. Well, they said with his jaw broken we won't be able to talk to him till this afternoon. I assumed you researched him."

"Actually, we were late getting up this morning because of the commotion in the middle of the night. I was just telling Melanie Thomas about our adventure while drinking coffee to wake up. I did a slight bit of research on him before I went to sleep last night, but nothing out of the ordinary. What did you hear back from your lieutenant who had dinner with the Treasury Department last night?

"They have been quietly suspicious of the security force at the Bureau of Printing and Engraving. They've been putting together a plan to investigate, but there's a lot at stake. International stock markets react to the US treasury. So if they went public that they suspected their security force of stealing multiple currency plates, there are consequences to that kind of announcement. After that, the lieutenant explained the case that your group is investigating, and he did some research on you. He would like to meet you and whatever is left of your team in about an hour. Can you get there?"

"Of course. Will you be joining us?"

"Fortunately, yes. As I was an eyewitness to our entry into the Bureau, their small investigative group is interested in talking to me."

"Give me the address and we'll be there in an hour."

The call ended and Jill did quick research on where the building was located. She and Madison would take the Metro so they wouldn't have to deal with parking. She would instruct Melanie in the security system just to make sure she was safe.

An hour later, she and Madison walked into the building for the scheduled meeting. It said 'Department of Treasury' on top. Many of the government buildings in Washington DC were impressive in their stateliness, and this building was no exception. Once inside, someone at an information desk sent them through an airport-like scanner, and then escorted them to a meeting room on the third floor. Jill recognized Detective Chambers and no one else when they entered the conference room.

They closed the door and sat about describing concerns with the security force at the Bureau.

Jill was never shy and decided to get her questions in early and often. "Do you know if there are any missing currency plates?"

"That's actually why this division came to our attention. We're missing currency plates for our ten-, twenty-, and hundred-dollar denominations. At any given time, someone is trying to create counterfeit US currency, but we haven't had an internal effort in nearly one hundred years. We don't know how many people are involved in the theft, but it has to include the Security division. Employees are required to go through a search upon each entry to and exit from the Bureau. The failure to detect three-foot by three-foot metal plates for currency printing is 100% the responsibility of the Security division. However, there are over one hundred employees in that department. While we might think about just eliminating the whole department and starting over, we have some honest people who would get caught in that. Furthermore, we wouldn't recover the plates. Recovering the plates has to be part of our strategy," said Ron Fisher, the seeming leader of the Treasury staff in the conference room.

"I have a pretty sophisticated team that helps me with these investigations and we began investigating the Security division last evening. My team has since departed for their homes in Wisconsin, but I can share that at least fifteen employees have suspicious deposits in their accounts."

"We'd like to see that information. Can you connect your laptop to our projector so we can share your findings with this room?"

"I can do that. Do you have any motives for Mr. Thomas's death in all of this? That is, after all, why I am on this case."

"We don't. Sadly, we were unaware of his death until my dinner meeting last night with your lieutenant. That finding paints this group as a much darker organization than we originally thought."

"This appears to be a group bent on insurrection. They want to overturn the federal government. It's interesting that many of them are employed by the federal government and it wouldn't be in their best interest to lose their paychecks. Of course, groups like this often lack critical thinking. When we researched the group, it almost felt like a Ponzi scheme, and that the leaders at the top were getting rich in their salary, and all they had to do was spout conspiracy theories to rile up the members of the group," Jill said.

"That's another piece of information I would like to hear about. Tell me all about this group and their relation to the Bureau of Printing and Engraving."

Jill took a final few moments to make the connection between her laptop and the screen projector and then began bringing up documents. Twenty minutes later, she had the attention of the group. They were amazed at what her team could research legally on the employees if one knew where to look.

After another hour of discussion, Jill returned to her original question: "What was the motive for killing Ed Thomas?"

"I think we'll have to take a look at the cutting machine and understand its relationship to the plates. He's not doing something on the job in the production of currency that would be especially interesting to a counterfeit organization. The plates are not in the machine when the sheets are being cut into individual bills. It's not like he was at the station that used the plates and could walk off with them."

"This might be your answer. According to his personnel record, he was able to operate several machines in the manufacturing area including the one using the plates. Many of the staff are cross-trained on several machines so that the manufacturing of currency isn't slowed down due to employee absences," Fisher said. "We don't have a record, however, of how recently he operated the plate machinery."

"Okay," Jill said, thinking.

"However, there was a rumor in the department that he stole the plate to fund his daughter's start-up company," Fisher added.

"That is absolutely not true. He funded his daughter's loan by borrowing against his retirement fund. This is something most parents would consider for their children. I wouldn't be surprised if he mentioned it at some point to his co-workers. I wonder if people gossiped about that to the point that his story got twisted, or did someone twist his story to put pressure on him to steal a plate? To the best of my knowledge, he didn't steal any plates. Mr. Fisher, do you have any information to the contrary about that?"

"I don't, but I'm interested in your verification of Ed Thomas's loan. I'd like to shut the door on that rumor."

Jill did a quick search, found the information from Jo about the loan, and put it on the screen.

Fisher nodded and said, "Door slammed shut on that piece of gossip."

"So we're back to examining the security staff at a minimum as they had to allow the plate to leave the building. My team developed a list of about one hundred security staff and . . ."

Fisher cut Jill off and asked, "How? How could you do that?"

"I have a great team. They did a search of various social media channels and developed the list in less than two hours. My financial person took the list and said that fifteen of the original group had suspicious financial transactions."

"Dr. Quint, you're making my head explode. I'm astounded at the data your team created in so little time."

"We've been at this for several years doing death investigations. Furthermore, my friends do similar work in their daytime jobs and they are really good."

"We're going to have to change our processes here. I'd love to interview your team members after we resolve this case. I think we could put more safeguards in place for employees who work in sensitive areas."

"Once we find Mr. Thomas's murderer, I'll be happy to share

their contact information with you. This murder is my top priority, while your top priority is finding the missing plates. I haven't figured out the connection yet between these two. The letter writing is very strange as well."

Detective Chambers shared the letters their victim and now his daughter received. Then they described their search of the Bureau. After a few questions and answers, there was silence in the conference room while Mr. Fisher and staff contemplated the new information.

"So we have a conspiracy group that may or may not be the right one—there are over sixty organizations in the United States that we are aware of, and you are right to be unsure that you have picked the right group. Did your social media maven, as I believe you called her, say if there was a connection between the security squad and the one conspiracy group that you have your eye on?" Fisher asked Jill.

"I don't believe so, as we ran out of time. She's back on her day job, but maybe Madison here can check that out as she's learning the social media maven's tricks," Jill said, looking at Madison. She caught a brief glimpse of panic on her intern's face knowing what a tall order it was to do what Marie could do, but she took a deep breath and nodded.

Mostly to take the focus off of Madison, she asked, "If you have the plates, can you produce currency that is not detected as counterfeit?"

"The average retail person can't detect it. We do recommend the use of counterfeit pens. When a clerk uses a highlighter on a bigger-denomination bill, it changes color if the correct ink has been used. So even if they have the plates, they still need the right ink and paper. So they won't pass the smell test, but they will be able to circulate some money."

Madison popped her head up and said, "The first security person of the suspicious fifteen is aligned to that one group. I'll work on the remaining."

"Okay then, we have a connection. So the next question is, can we make a link between the executives of the 7% and the payments the security force received. Mr. Fisher, you must have some forensic accountants in the Treasury Department to follow the money between these two groups."

"I do. In fact, my colleague here on my right, Ms. Sutherland, is a forensic accountant. While we have been discussing this case, she's been verifying your colleague's information. I'm happy to reveal that it is accurate."

"Of course it is," Jill said. "You do realize that besides working with several law-enforcement agencies in the US, we have also assisted Interpol and the Italian police on tracking money. My friend is a licensed CPA. She may not be a licensed forensic accountant, but I'll bet on her before anyone else in the world. Talk to Detective Chambers; he verified my team's actions and information with the FBI," Jill said, tired of having to prove herself and her team's capabilities over and over.

"My apologies, Dr. Quint. Call me a cynic as I have met many federal contractors who had little substance behind their bravado. You appear to be one of the few with substance. I wanted to add that Ms. Sutherland followed your colleague's process and investigated other staff operating production machinery in the Bureau, and she has found some of the same irregular deposits as you found in the security staff."

"Yes, it can't be just one division or another at the Bureau, or the plan to steal plates wouldn't work. One more question—does the Bureau keep spare plates on hand? I toured the Fort Worth, Texas, currency facility and I know you have people who check the quality of the bill sheets after they come off the press. When a plate wears out, I assume there are spare plates stored somewhere so your maintenance people can pop the old plate out and the new one in when there is a quality issue with the current plate. I can't see you shutting production down until someone makes a new plate for you. So are the plates missing from the machine or from storage? Is there a twenty-four-hour shift at the Bureau, or could the night-time security staff steal the plates when no one is around?"

Madison looked up and said, "I've verified that ten of our fifteen suspects so far belong to the 7%. I have five people to go. I will say that these are all male names and my research says that we should see some women involved in this group. Women comprise about 14% of far-right extremist groups per a 2022 study. While I investigate this final five, maybe Mr. Fisher could say something about the role of women at the Bureau of Printing and Engraving."

Jill received a text on her phone and looked down. "We've got to go; there's another attempt at breaking into our apartment," Jill said as she and then Madison began collecting their belongings to leave.

"I'll come with you," Detective Chambers said.

"Actually, can you drive? We took the subway here."

CHAPTER 13

"Normally, I wouldn't use my siren for a routine burglary, but nothing about your location is likely routine," Detective Chambers said.

"Thank you," Jill said, worried about Melanie.

Madison texted from the back seat.

This is an exciting ride!! My head is about to explode with all I've learned from you on this case. Wow.

Jill looked back and smiled. Between the noise inside the car and a lack of desire to distract the detective, it wasn't the time to be talking.

She texted Melanie that they were on their way, but got no response. It was doubtful that their client was asleep as she'd had a good night's sleep. In no time, they pulled up to the building and the detective double-parked at the front entrance. Jill ran inside the lobby and saw the elevator door about to close. She blocked it and waited briefly as Madison and Detective Chambers were on her heels. She punched the button for her floor and soon they were racing down the hallway to the apartment.

The detective put out an arm and said, "Let me go first. I'm the cop."

He directed the two women to stay behind either side of the doorframe, then announced, "Police are entering this apartment."

He stayed at the door and listened. They could hear both a male and a female voice in the back of the apartment. He stuck his head inside the door and quickly looked around. Seeing that the coast was clear, he entered. He considered telling Dr. Quint and her assistant to stay outside in the hallway, but from what he observed, he would be wasting his time and breath. He found no one in the kitchen or living room of the apartment and so he crept silently toward the room with the voices. As he approached the room, he debated identifying himself again and decided not to. He could feel Dr. Quint practically breathing down his neck. He knew he was the only person with a gun among the three of them. He stopped and listened again.

"Why won't you tell me where you put the plates?" said the male voice. "We know your father has them, but he wouldn't pass them over."

"How do you know that he has plates? Did you see him walk out with them? I frequently visited my Dad at his house and he never mentioned that he had them."

Jill took notes on what the man was saying. Madison had her phone on record. The detective briefly peered into the room to get eyes on Melanie to make sure she wasn't in danger. He leaned in and stuck one eyeball beyond the door frame and then moved back. He held up his hand in an okay symbol. Jill relaxed a little knowing that Melanie didn't have a knife to her throat.

"Look, you broke into this apartment and I've told you that I don't have what you're looking for. You need to leave."

"I know you have the plates. Just give them to me."

"I don't have the plates. Who told you that I have them?"

"What do you mean who told me? We all know that your father stole the plates and then sold them to fund your new company."

"Okay, I don't know who told you that, but they're lying. That's not how my company was funded."

"Well, we searched your apartment and your father's, so I'm going to search this apartment and then I'll leave."

Detective Chambers had enough. He reached behind his back for the ubiquitous handcuffs and entered the bedroom that Melanie was using.

"Sir, you are under arrest for breaking and entering into a building." The detective was about to read the man his rights, but he made a dash for the door and Jill swung her computer bag at him while Madison held her foot out, tripping him.

The detective approached the downed man and handcuffed him. As soon as he was secured, he called for backup.

"What's your name?" Jill asked, while Madison entered Melanie's bedroom to give the woman a hug.

"None of your business."

"Who told you that Ed Thomas stole plates?"

"I'm not saying anything."

"We'll have your identity soon, so you may as well tell me your name," Detective Chambers said.

"No you won't, I don't have any identification on me."

Chambers laughed. "Is that what your fellow 7 Percenters said would keep you safe from the police? We'll just fingerprint you when we get down to the station."

"Actually, when you get him on his feet, I'll take his picture and run it through my facial-identity program. We'll know who you are before you leave this apartment."

Jill decided his face was in a good position and leaned over his torso to take a close picture. She gathered up the computer bag that she slugged him with and returned to the kitchen to open the laptop and check his photograph.

Within a minute, she called out "His name is Jeremy Pons. He's a resident of Virginia. He did military service; he's had one DUI conviction, but no other criminal activity."

"I continue to be amazed by you, Dr. Quint. Would you send that information to me via text or email?"

She hit a few buttons on her laptop and said, "Done."

She heard a knocking at the door and a call out of "Police, we're responding to a request from Detective Chambers."

Jill let the officers in and Detective Chambers had one of the officers read Jeremy his rights so it could be caught on the body camera the officers were wearing. They got him to his feet and were about to exit the apartment.

"Is there any chance I could watch your interview with him?" Jill asked.

"No, but I'm not surprised you asked. I'll let you know what he says. Thank you for the quick identification. You may want to move Melanie again. We could probably find a safe location for her. Let me know what you want to do. There are more of these men out there, and as soon as they learn that Jeremy is in our custody, they'll send someone else."

"I know. I'll talk it over with her and let you know."

Soon the apartment was quiet and Jill went back to where Madison and Melanie were sitting on the side of the bed in her room.

"Are you doing okay, Melanie?" Jill asked.

"Yes. I knew the alarm had gone off, and that you would be here soon. I didn't see that he was carrying a weapon, so I didn't feel like my life was in danger."

"The detective thinks that they will try again. These people are convinced that your father stole a plate to finance your company. So someone obviously told a lot of gossip at the Bureau of Printing and Engraving. The detective offered to move you to a safe house as both he and I think they'll be back."

"I'm doing okay here, so I think I'll stay. Maybe I'll start going out with you guys when you leave to do something related to the case. I can always carry my laptop with me and get some work done nearby."

"Yeah, or you could randomly find a coffee house that's crowded and work there. They seem to be going after you only when you're alone. Someone must have watched us leave this building and knew you were here by yourself."

"I was in the kitchen working on my laptop when I heard scratching at the front door. So I ran back to the bedroom and texted you, even though I was sure the alarm was going to work. It went off for a few minutes and then he found me in the bedroom and asked me to turn it off. Since my ears were about to fall off my head and I was sure you knew I needed help, I did. These guys are screwy in their thinking. They must have gossiped about Dad at work. I wonder if they targeted him as the thief because they knew he was helping me with my company? It feels like they wished it to be true and so it was. However, from what you said, someone really did steal the plates and gave them to someone else to do something with them. Someone in their organization is not admitting to having the plates in their possession and they are keeping the focus on me and my father. Why?"

"That's a good question. Those CEOs were paying themselves well at the top. I wonder if they had possession of the plates and sold them to someone else for more income on the side; then they could keep even more money for themselves. I think it's time to focus my attention on them."

"We should also circle back to the Treasury people who were in that conference room to see if they have new discoveries," Madison said.

"Yes. Let's have lunch and see what we can learn while we surf the net."

They made sandwiches and Jill took one of the executives and Madison the other. They took notes and then planned to talk when they were done. Jill paused a moment, thinking about the weirdness of having their client live with them, but then let it go.

She was ready to discuss with Madison a while later. "This is much more complicated than I expected." Jill said.

"I agree. From everything I could find, these executives are also members of a local crime family—the Cottonne Family," Madison said. "Can I just add WTH! How did this go from a simple case of proving someone didn't die of a heart attack to stolen bodies, militia groups, counterfeit currency, and now the mafia? Or do we call it Organized Crime?"

Jill laughed and said, "This is what I call a case going sideways. It starts as something very simple and then morphs into this monster case." Jill checked to see if Melanie was listening, but she had earbuds in and was clear on the other side of the large room talking with someone. "What's more, we are down to a few days to solve it. That's when the client's money runs out."

"I'm learning so much from this investigation. If we don't solve it, I'd like to pull from my trust fund to keep us on the job. For one thing, I'm getting a full sixteen hours a day of training that goes toward my requirement. Can you put more hours on the case if you're funded?"

"I have a few more days beyond that, but I have a feeling it will break open by then," Jill said with a confident smile.

"Really? That's good news. Why do you think it's going to break open?"

"When you've been on as many cases as I have, you just get this feeling of momentum gathering, and I sort of feel that way at the moment."

Madison looked at her mentor and whispered, not wanting their client to hear just in case she was trying at the moment, "How do you get that gut feeling? I feel like we know more, but we don't have a motive and we have many unknowns. There seem to be men watching us and breaking into wherever Melanie is to look for the plates. How could we be close to a breakthrough?"

"In my experience, criminals get impatient. Do you remember the case in Asheville? If our suspect and her family avoided going after you and lighting your house on fire, they would have stayed hidden much longer. It's sort of the same here. If they would have just killed Ed Thomas and not torn apart his apartment and Melanie's, we would be missing critical pieces of information to understand the case."

"Do you know who the murderer is?"

"No, but just remember at the start of this case it could have been millions of people. Now we're down to a group of less than one hundred. That's real progress even though it doesn't feel like it. I think the murderer is going to come from one of two groups, and the two groups may intersect. It's either someone from the Security division at the Bureau or someone from the 7% group."

"How about the mafia? How are they involved, and why aren't you labeling them as the potential murderers?"

"I think the mafia is connected at the highest level. The order may have come from them, but the actual interception of the Chinese food came from an underling. Sometimes in these cases for the good of your community or just mankind, you have to go further than identifying the murderer. You need to take down the organization that made that underling do what he or she did."

"True. So what are our next steps?"

Jill had been checking her text messages while she was working on the dossier for the two leaders. She was pleased and really not surprised to get a text from her husband, Nathan, that he had just landed at the airport and he asked for the address of her lodgings.

"First, I'm going downstairs as Nathan is about to arrive by taxi to this building. After I spend a few moments reuniting with him, we'll call Detective Chambers to discuss our latest findings and see if they learned anything from the man who was removed from here."

"That's really cool how he rearranges his schedule to help you on a case," Madison said.

"He only occasionally helps me on a case. His presence,

though, brings security. I don't have to keep my guard up because he's my guard. That allows me to focus on the problem at hand which is, "Who killed Ed Thomas?" With that, Jill grabbed the apartment key and went down to the lobby.

CHAPTER 14

She reached the door just as Nathan was approaching with a duffle bag on his shoulder. She opened the door for him and he dropped his bag, and bent for a hug and kiss.

"I never would have asked you to come, but I'm glad you're here. I was just explaining to Madison that I can relax when you're around as I know you have my back and I don't have to devote some of my brain energy to watching for killers at every turn."

"I missed you and I miss being on the periphery of an investigation. Even though we talked and you gave me updates, there's nothing like watching you work."

"Ha! Though I admit that I like watching you create new labels and your reasons for colors, items, and words on a label. I guess we both like watching each other's brain work. Weird, huh?"

They reached the apartment door and Jill paused to tell Nathan what had happened while he was on the airplane and in particular that their client was being harassed when she was left alone. Likely someone watched Nathan arrive and Jill greet him, as that was the way things were going at the moment. Nathan nodded and entered the large apartment, setting down his bags.

He greeted Madison on the way to be introduced to Melanie. She looked up from her computer screen and pulled off a headset.

"Hey Melanie, this is my husband Nathan. He just arrived from California. He'll be added protection to keep us all safe. He's also a great cook, so be prepared for some excellent food and wine pairings."

Nathan spent a few moments chatting with Melanie and then moved back to where Jill and Madison were talking. He grabbed his bags and Jill showed him which bedroom was theirs, leaving him to get settled.

When he returned she asked, "Did you have lunch already? We have sandwich fixings in the refrigerator. I really need to call the detective with our latest finding and see if I can get another meeting with his folks."

"I didn't come here to slow down your investigation. I'll fend for myself and you call the detective."

"Thanks, Sweetie," Jill said, giving him a hug of appreciation. She wrote a few notes to herself of what she wanted to cover and made the call.

"Dr. Quint, I was just about to call you. This simple homicide is turning into the most complex case I've ever seen. Are you available for another meeting today with an expanded group from this morning's meeting?"

"Sure. I have some new information for you as well, Detective. Do you want me to share now or just head out for the meeting?"

"As much as I would love to hear what new information you have, this next meeting is happening at the FBI headquarters here in the District. Do you know where that is?"

"I do. I'll head there now. May I bring my assistant, Madison?"

"It's better to ask forgiveness than permission. I won't remember your asking that question."

"Thank you. See you in a few."

She ended the call and said, "Sweetie, Madison and I are needed at FBI HQ. Sorry to run off when you just got here."

"No worries. I'll keep Melanie safe."

"Don't hesitate to call 911 if you hear someone trying to break in. So far they haven't been armed, but there's a first time for everything."

He nodded with his head stuck in the refrigerator. Jill and Madison left the apartment after quickly determining that the metro was the fastest way to reach the Hoover Building which housed the FBI.

About 20 minutes later, they walked into a conference room in the Hoover Building that was filled with even more people. They were handed paper nameplates and asked to write their names on them and place them in front of them and sign a confidentiality contract. Jill had met with the FBI on other cases—in fact, she had a good friend who was the San Francisco special agent in charge. She recognized a few familiar faces from the morning's meeting, but most were new faces. Those new faces displayed acronyms on their nameplates, some of which Jill could figure out and others which were a complete mystery.

It seemed that she and Madison were the last to arrive, and as soon as they settled, introductions began. "This is rather an odd meeting, in that we have civilians with us. However, Dr. Quint comes with a reputation with Interpol, the FBI, and our District police. I'd like everybody to introduce themselves and include whatever acronym or agency you're with. Dr. Quint, let's start with you." The man who spoke had a nameplate that said James Davis with one of those acronyms underneath.

Jill took the opportunity to introduce herself and Madison. She gave a brief work history, including those prior experiences with the agencies the leader of the meeting had mentioned. Given the testosterone in the room, she doubted that it made a differ- ence for some people, but she didn't care; it was all part of the job, and at least they were included in the room. Once the introduc- tions finished, the focus was on Jill, and she was asked to summa- rize the case.

"I was contacted by the daughter of an employee of the Bureau of Printing and Engraving named Ed Thomas. She said he was in otherwise good health, but authorities said he died of a heart attack on the job. When I arrived, the local medical examiner would not invite me to the autopsy. That is their purview to make the decision. They finished examining Mr. Thomas's remains, and I was making arrangements for a second autopsy at his designated funeral home. It was at that point that his remains were stolen from the medical examiner's office by a fake mortuary team. Perhaps twenty-four hours later, his remains were found on a roadside in Virginia. During that interim, the ME's office received test results revealing that he had the poison ricin in his blood and that was the cause of his death. His routine delivery of Chinese food contained the poison, and the restaurant said that two separate delivery people arrived for the meal about two minutes apart. This became a homicide for the District police.

"I have a team that supports me that is capable of doing background checks, social media evaluations, and facial-recognition software, as well as a forensic accountant to follow the money as that is often a confounding factor."

Jill named the software company founded by her friend, Henrik Klein, and she saw some nods around the room at the name recognition. She also saw people taking notes which told her they were listening and evaluating her words.

"There has been a break-in at the victim's house as well as that of his daughter. The burglars are looking for missing currency plates. While our victim wasn't working the machine that has plates in it, he has in the past and is knowledgeable of that machine. Those two burglars are in custody of the District police and I'll leave it to Detective Chambers to describe any interview results. There was a rumor in the Bureau that our victim had stolen a plate to fund his daughter's start-up company. I can verify for you that is not true. He took out a loan against his pension to fund his daughter's company.

"We believe that there is a militia group called the 7% behind this murder and the search for currency plates. My recent research which I haven't shared yet with the detective suggests that organized crime is also involved. The very well paid executives of the militia group are also members of the Cottonne Organized Crime family. It appears from my research that they are using militia dues and other activities to further the interests of the crime family, but we're just starting our research into that connection.

"I understand that there are missing currency plates at the Bureau. My research also shows that approximately fifteen of the hundred employees that work in the security division at the Bureau have had suspicious payments into their bank accounts and some of these people belong to this militia group. To steal a three-foot by three-foot metal plate would take the cooperation of the Security force to get it out of the Bureau. It's simply too large to be hidden in something."

Jill paused for a moment to take a sip of water from the bottled water in front of her. "Here is what I don't know: I don't know who Ed Thomas's murderer is. I don't know how many currency plates are missing from the Bureau. I don't have a motive for his murder. There's a connection between Ed and members of the 7% militia group that goes back over twenty years ago to his military service. My suspect list is down to about thirty people, but I'll be off this case in a few days."

"Thank you for that thorough explanation, Dr. Quint. I think we all learned something new in this room. Let me now give you some new information. As a reminder, you signed a confidentiality agreement at the door. You may not relay anything you learn in this room including to Melanie Thomas, who is your employer on this investigation." He waited for Madison and Jill to acknowledge their understanding and then he continued.

Jill gave a brief thought to the awkward position this information put her in. Melanie was her client, but as long as she made progress with the case, she needn't tell her everything.

"What we didn't tell you at the start is this is a secret task force aware of the Cottonne Family, the 7%, and the missing plates at the Bureau. Also, your victim, Ed Thomas, was working undercover for us. At the appropriate time, we'll let his daughter know of his heroism."

There was dead silence in the room, and then Jill asked, "Were you aware at the start that he was murdered?"

"Yes."

Jill heard a few mumblings around her, and she said, "At the very least, you need to reimburse Melanie Thomas for the work my team has done on this case. You wasted her time, money, and her emotions."

Jill was furious. She felt like she was set up by these idiots with no concern for Melanie's loss.

"Actually, one of the reasons you're here is we have a contract offer for you and your assistant," said Davis.

Jill had a range of emotions. She felt like a fool researching the case when a secret government committee knew all about it. She had a duty to Melanie, and she didn't trust these people. Melanie had been threatened and where were these people? They left her unprotected.

"Look, I don't trust you people. Where have you been when my client was under attack from these militia men? You didn't even tell the police department that Ed's death was a homicide. Somehow in your zeal to infiltrate this organization and your desire for secrecy, you've ignored the risks to innocent bystanders like Melanie Thomas."

Jill had a juvenile desire to stand up and pull on her hair as this secret task force was driving her crazy.

James Davis said, "The accusations you hurled at us are for the most part accurate. We didn't think they would go after our informant. We certainly didn't foresee them going after his daughter.

We will be approaching Miss Thomas and attempt to move her to protective custody."

"At some point you're going to have to bring her in on the bigger picture. As I mentioned earlier, you certainly need to reimburse her for the expense of hiring me, and I'll be happy to give you a detailed accounting of that. So, among this group of organized criminals and militia men, do you have a murderer in mind?" Jill asked. She was still mad, but her overall feeling was a deep curiosity behind whoever poisoned Ed's food with ricin.

"Dr. Quint, does this mean you'll agree to join our task force and sign the contract that I've laid out for you?"

"For me to be most effective, I need to use my team members for some of my research. My forensic accountant taught Interpol's forensic accountants some new techniques to look for information—that's just how good she is. If organized crime is involved, then beyond family loyalty it's all about money. Do you have a forensic accountant on your task force?"

"We do, and we don't. We have someone assigned to us, but your group managed to dig out more information."

"If you've done your research on my team, then you know that they have day jobs in Wisconsin but would be willing to do some work on this case for me. What is your plan—tie my hands and not have the best resources available, or can I read them into the situation after they sign your confidentiality agreement?"

Jill heard a sigh from the man at the head of the table. He apparently walked in thinking that she would be thrilled to work with his brilliant team. But this wasn't her first rodeo, and she knew how to negotiate to get the things she wanted. Then her cell phone buzzed. She read the text.

"I've got to go; my apartment is being broken into again. Fortunately, my husband just arrived from California and he's a Master Black Belt in Hapkido, so Melanie will have good protection. Detective, would you like to join me again?" Jill and Madison got up to leave as did Detective Chambers. Then she looked around the room and said, "There's room for all of you if you would like to continue the conversation and perhaps explain to Melanie Thomas what is happening before you assist her into protective custody. I'll sign your contract for services there."

Jill wrote the address down, gave it to James Davis, and rushed out with Madison and the detective who again, thankfully had a car nearby.

"That was an interesting bit of strategy work there, Jill. Do you think they'll follow you here?"

"Maybe not all of them, perhaps just James Davis and one other person to assist Melanie. He's the leader and the others in the room were not contributing to this investigation during the meeting, other than taking notes. However, I'm not always right. I was really mad at the emotional distress they've put Melanie through. Her father's volunteering to be undercover was his decision, but what has happened since is on them."

"I feel like I should be getting bonus hours for all that I'm learning in this case," Madison said. "Just wow!"

"Are you sure you want to get your P.I. license? As you can see, there are horrible bureaucracies to deal with as well as people with large egos. Just remember why you're hired—to bring justice to the clients and their family members."

"Actually, my involvement in this case is cementing my desire to become a P.I."

"Also remember, you're likely going to have a lot of boring surveillance cases before you get exciting cases. Given my expertise, I only get called in for homicides. If someone did see my P.I. license and ask me to do surveillance, that would be a firm 'no,' but you don't have my background and years of experience," Jill said as they pulled up to her apartment building in a police car for the second time that day.

CHAPTER 15

The three of them rushed into the building and took the elevator to their floor. They approached the door with speed, then slowed once the detective held up his hand indicating that he would take the lead. They listened and heard no sounds, but the door was ajar. They pushed it open, and Jill heard Nathan call out, "Come in, it's safe."

"That's my husband speaking."

Still the detective looked around the corner into the apartment slowly. Then he stood to his full height and walked in. They found Melanie and Nathan in the living room, with a man on the floor between them, tied up with the duct tape that Jill had left on the counter from the earlier encounter.

Jill rushed over to where he was seated, hugged him, then said, "Nathan, what happened?"

"This man has no identification on him and hasn't told us his name, but he walked into the apartment after doing something to the door. He then walked over to Melanie who was on her computer working. She looked up and told him to get out. He asked her something, then I kicked his head and he fell to the floor. While he was down there I decided to secure him and wait for your arrival rather than calling 911. He's regained his wits, but he's not talking. I searched his clothing for a wallet, but I didn't find one. I was tempted to try your facial-recognition thing, but I don't know how that works. I did take a photo, which I sent you."

The detective placed his handcuffs on the man and then called for some uniforms to escort the man to jail.

Jill pulled her laptop out of the bag she'd taken to the meeting and went to work identifying the man. Moments later she had a name.

"This is John Paul Minton. He's a resident of Virginia."

There was a knock on the door and two uniformed officers entered the apartment to get their suspect on his feet and haul him away. Detective Chambers followed them out.

"How are you doing, Melanie?" Jill asked.

She sighed and replied, "With your husband here, I knew I was never in any danger. I looked up a video on YouTube and saw the moves that a martial artist like him can do. There seems to be an endless supply of earnest young misguided men who are sure that I have the plates. I feel like I should head west to get away from them."

There was another knock on the door. Jill looked through the peephole in the door and recognized James Davis. There were other people with him, but Jill couldn't identify them through the small hole. She opened the door.

"Mr. Davis, won't you come in?"

After the three people entered the apartment, Jill said to Melanie, "These are some of the people I was in a meeting with when I got the notice that the alarm was going off. Why don't you people introduce yourself to Melanie Thomas?" Jill said, mindful of the confidentiality agreement and not wanting to say the wrong thing.

After introductions were made, and Nathan reiterated the events with John Paul Minton, Jill waited in silence to see what

James Davis was going to do. Would he live up to her expectation that he come clean with Melanie, or would he continue his charade with the victim's daughter?

Perhaps, after assessing the danger of an endless number of men visiting this apartment to find the currency plates, he made up his mind to reveal some of the information to Melanie.

He produced a confidentiality agreement for Melanie and Nathan to sign. Then he offered a somewhat limited explanation of his committee's work and his desire to place Melanie in protective custody. When she heard about her father doing undercover work, tears began streaming down her face. Madison fetched a tissue box and put an arm around the girl. After she packed her possessions, she left the apartment with two of the people who had arrived with Davis.

Nathan said to Jill, "Can't you ever have a simple homicide case?"

"Apparently not. Madison even said that she should be credited for double the hours of private detective training, because so much was going on with this case."

Nathan smiled at Jill and then asked, "How are you going to get the word out to this militia group that Melanie is no longer here, and there's no point in searching this apartment or her house for the plates?"

"I asked the two people who are escorting Melanie to pause a few seconds outside and make sure that anybody watching this building gets a glimpse of her. I also asked them to stop by her apartment so she could pick up her things and to alert anybody lurking in her neighborhood that she is not staying there. My people are armed, but so far your burglars haven't tried to physically attack any people," Davis said.

"Mostly, that's because we've disabled them. However, none of them have had knives or guns on their person. I hope for both their sakes and ours that continues to be their pattern."

"It's the difference between being charged with a misdemeanor and a felony. They'll likely be charged with trespassing rather than aggravated assault. Since several of your trespassers ended up in bad shape after encountering you, they'll likely be released immediately so the prison system doesn't have to pay their medical bills."

Jill thought about that and said, "I like that idea. One guy has a broken jaw and another has a concussion, and rather than the taxpayers footing their bills, they'll have to pay for them out of their own insurance. If we get any more trespassers, I'll have to see if I can keep breaking jaws."

"How did you break someone's jaw? Are you a martial arts expert, too?" Davis asked.

"I'm in the early stage of the martial arts journey. When we had our first visitor, I took the lampshade off a lamp. I caught the guy just as he was entering my bedroom and I swung the lamp base like I had the potential for a homerun. That uppercut broke the man's jaw. Whoops."

"Who needs martial arts when you have lamps?" Nathan said.

"Actually, I like the thought of these men having their jaws wired shut for a few weeks. It's a fitting punishment and likely makes it hard to participate in militia activities if you can't talk."

"Alrighty then, getting back on track. Are you now willing to sign our contract to assist us with breaking up this group and getting the currency plates returned to the Bureau?"

"I'm ready to help you find Ed Thomas's murderer and break up this militia group and its organized crime backers."

"That's what I said," Davis said.

Jill read the contract, then decided it was worthy of signing. She debated what to advise Madison. "With the contract I've signed, I could hire you as an employee. However, thinking of your résumé, you would be better off signing a separate contract with the FBI, and then in the future you can claim you were consulted by them. That will give you street cred with clients."

Madison nodded and read the contract. She then signed it and took a picture of each page for her records.

Jill smiled to herself that the young private detective in training was living her dream and she was happy for her.

With the paperwork completed, they got down to business. "Why did you ask Ed Thomas to be an undercover agent for you?"

"The problem goes back perhaps eighteen months. Leadership at the Bureau of Printing and Engraving knew they had a problem. Never in recent history had a currency plate gone missing. The leaders quickly concluded that there was no way to get currency plates out of the Bureau other than having the security personnel be a part of it. That's a serious deficiency for them to handle internally."

"How did the leaders discover the missing plate?" Jill asked.

"They were notified by the vendor that makes plates of an unusual replacement of an existing plate. The leader actually went down to the production area to count plates. That was when the large-bill plates were discovered missing. There was a spare kept for each currency because they didn't want production to stop until a new plate was manufactured. Plates take a few days to make. The leader contacted the FBI as we deal with counterfeit currency investigations. He also wanted to avoid internal channels as he saw them as compromised."

"Knowing that you can limit your focus to one hundred security employees is helpful, but not much," Jill said.

"Yes. Finding the thief was one thing, but knowing where the plates were and what the plans for these plates are is even more critical. There have been many counterfeiting attempts throughout our history, but at least in the last hundred years they have not been carried out with the Bureau's authentic currency plates. A counterfeiter needs three things to be successful—the plates, the paper, and the ink. The easiest to detect is a poor currency plate. The impact to world markets if the problem of counterfeit US currency is made public is substantial."

"So how did Ed Thomas come into your equation?"

"We spent considerable time doing background checks on the Bureau's employees. It was at that time that we discovered membership of clusters of employees in the 7% militia. We used our Behavioral Analysis Unit to understand the situation."

"That's a good choice of a tool. I have a forensic psychologist whom I can call on in California, but I didn't think of using her in this case. I guess the question is: Why do these men join this militia group? It sort of has a cult feeling to me."

"Exactly. You mentioned that your research revealed that the top leaders of the militia group were members of the Cottonne Organized Crime family. That was new information to us. It's also new information to feed to our BAU. Militias can be bad enough on their own without combining resources with a crime family."

"Frankly, I was blown away by the pay of these top executives, so we did an in-depth search of their backgrounds and a financial analysis of the group. It was approved as a nonprofit by the Internal Revenue Service. The militia's primary source of income is dues. These executives operate both a local chapter and a national organization with their militia. They mainly seem to stir the pot—make enough outrageous statements to keep random acts of violence going—while not endangering themselves by participating," Jill said.

"These militia groups often have ex-military members, and several contacted Ed to become a member of the group. Some of those men served with him and thought for sure he would join, but he wasn't impressed with their pitch or what the militia stood for. He thought they were fake soldiers unable to move on from their military service and function in a changing world—those are his exact words. He heard whispered conversations in the break room and around the manufacturing area and he was concerned. He'd kept in touch with someone else from his military service who works in the FBI. He explained the problem he was hearing about at work and at just about the time we were brought in by the leadership to deal with a potential counterfeit problem. As they say, it was a perfect match."

"Until Ed was murdered."

"Yes," was Davis's somber reply.

Good, thought Jill. He knew they had lost a good and honorable man in this operation of theirs.

"Do you have any suspects in mind to be Ed's murderer?"

"Short of suspecting the entire militia and most of the Bureau's employees, no."

"You also don't know who stole the plates and what their plans are?"

"No. Those plates could be used for counterfeiting, or they could be sold on the dark web to a high bidder, or they could end up in a third-world country that plans to disrupt the world's economy if the US dollar can't be trusted,"

"So you would like me and my team to find those answers soon and quietly."

"Yes."

"Okay. We'll see what we can do. One request, can you give Madison access to DC road cameras? I want to do some work there."

"I'll get that for you. This is an urgent situation. I would like to hear from you daily or sooner whenever you have new information. On the legal side, I will have to get warrants for arrest, haul in suspects etc."

"I know the drill," Jill replied. Her mind was elsewhere, conjuring a plan to attack both problems. Her first question was how soon she could get Marie, Jo, and Angela working with her. Her contract with the feds would cover travel costs, but she didn't think she needed them physically in the same room as her. She would have to find out what was going on in their day jobs to see if they could help her. First, though, she wanted to find Thomas's murderer.

James Davis departed their apartment once he felt he had the arrangement in place. He hated hiring civilian consultants. However, she had worked with other FBI offices, and came with strong recommendations. He felt his office could continue as is and eventually would solve the case, but the advice from his colleagues was to hire her and accelerate the rate at which it would be solved.

CHAPTER 16

$\mathcal{A}$fter the FBI agent left the room, Jill discussed her plan
with Madison and Nathan. While he normally wasn't
involved in her cases, she always welcomed his input as he often
thought of something she hadn't.

"Once you get access to the DC road cameras, I want you to
devote your time and attention to identifying the delivery guy
with the Chinese food. You've seen me use Henrik's software
system, and I think we can program it to search for the motorcyclist throughout the District. At some point he had to take his
helmet off and we'll get an identity at that point. If he left the
District and took the helmet off in Maryland or Virginia, then will
need to liaison with the FBI to get access to those road cameras
also."

"I wonder if we could use our same technology to track the
movement of those plates? We don't know when they left the
Bureau of Printing and Engraving, but we likely have a two-week
range. Oh, and I'll ask Mr. Davis to give us a picture of a plate. I
will see if we can capture anybody who's carrying it. It's a long-
shot, but it's our technology that will be working hard, not us, so
let's give that a try."

"Do you really think someone exited the building carrying a large metal plate?" Madison asked.

"I don't know. Perhaps they covered it in wrapping paper or put it in a box that perhaps the currency paper arrived in, but maybe they just boldly walked out of the building with the plates. Remember, some of these guys are not the sharpest tool in the shed, and they don't see manipulation when it's hitting them in the face. Maybe someone in the militia leadership asked them to walk out with the plate and so they did. I don't think we'll get that lucky, though, but it's worth a try."

Nathan looked at Jill and decided he should plan on doing what he usually did to support her. "I'm going to head out and go shopping for food and wine. I think you'll be hunkered down here for a few days, and that you'll have guests stopping in now and then for which you'll need beverages and snacks. However, given that this apartment has been attacked three times, perhaps I should draw up a list and have a service shop for me."

"We'll be fine. I've fended off these guys twice. Can you add vinegar and jalapeño peppers and a child's water gun to the shopping list?"

Madison was thinking about the pleasure of having someone cook for her. Especially someone rumored to be as good to cook as Nathan was. Was the water gun used to sprinkle some marinade over a dish?

Jill had been watching her intern think about what she had requested, she laughed out loud when she saw that Madison had reached the wrong conclusion.

"Madison, you know I hate to cook. I don't know anything about cooking. I won't be using a water gun for cooking. The deal I have with Nathan in our marriage is that I stay out of the kitchen. The water gun is so I can make a homemade concoction of pepper spray to nail the next burglar with a burning eye solution."

Madison switched direction quickly and said, "Beyond everything else you're teaching me, you'll have to give me the recipe for your pepper spray. Certainly you can't bring it with you on an airplane, and for all I know it's illegal to carry in certain parts of the United States. Far better to make your own concoction and use a children's toy to deliver it. I'll pass that on to my father. He's been worried about my personal safety. Given my chosen line of work, I could get a gun permit in North Carolina, but I would rather not as I'm not sure I could shoot someone dead. You have to be sure; otherwise, there's no point in carrying a gun. I'm absolutely sure I could aim a water gun and shoot anyone giving me a problem."

"Exactly. I'm guessing it's going to take an hour for the agent to give us access to the cameras. Let's talk about strategy for a while."

"I'm not familiar with poisons. Could this motorcycle rider open the takeout container of food and sprinkle it with, say, a tablespoon of ricin? Maybe stir it into the sauce? You're the toxicologist; how would you add the ricin to his food?"

"Ricin kills in small amounts so, yes, a tablespoon would do. Heat denatures the proteins and deactivates it as a poison. So if the person who made the ricin understood that, they would have the rider put it on the food just before it was delivered so the food's temperature would not deactivate the poison."

"Okay, that helps. Should we do any search for equipment to purify castor beans, or can anybody figure it out?" Madison asked.

"I would think you could make a concoction with standard kitchen equipment. You can't buy the beans generally on the internet, but you can plant the bush that makes castor beans anytime you want."

"Okay, I'll concentrate on the delivery person."

"I'm going to put a call in to my friends and see if they can help with understanding the Cottonne relationship to this militia."

"I did some early research on the subject. Organized crime has taken over neighborhoods and they operate their own security forces in most of Latin America. These criminals sell drugs, extort their citizens, and steal oil. The organizations themselves may no longer be families, but somehow they're related enough to form these criminal enterprises. That doesn't fit what we're seeing in the US, though certainly the mafia here has dealt with drugs and prostitution in its history."

"Okay, if I can get some of Marie and Jo's attention, I'm going to have them focus on the individuals as well as the family. We worked on a case in Sicily where the mafia was involved in the death of an American over a future business transaction. However, that's a very different mafia situation than what we have in the United States."

"Just wow! I can't wait to have a reputation that people want my help solving crimes around the world."

Jill smiled and reached out to her friends. Jo and Marie were available and were happy to hear of the pay coming their way for work on this case.

"The names of the three leaders of the militia are Thomas Poli, Michael Messina, and John Campanella. Respectively, they are president, vice-president, and treasurer of the 7% militia, but my research shows them as connected to the Cottonne Family. What can you tell me about this crime family? Why would they want to belong to a militia? Do they have a history of counterfeiting currency?"

"Jill, you land the most interesting murder cases. This started with a daughter not believing her father died of a heart attack, and now you've arrived at organized crime and counterfeiting. Let me dig into this information and I'll tell you what I find. I should have some answers in the next two to three hours," Jo said.

"I have to echo Jo's statement, and I think I'll have information on these three individuals in under an hour. Let me go to work," Marie said.

Jill ended her phone call and stared at her drawing of the murder and theft of currency plates. When Melanie was in the apartment, she hadn't hung her usual murder board on the wall. However, now that she was secure, Jill took tape and adhered it to the wall. She leaned against the couch, staring at it and trying to think of a new angle. Nathan had left the apartment to go shopping and Madison was using her laptop to make sure she understood the facial-recognition software before she began using it to search for the motorcyclist.

There was a sound of someone buzzing the apartment from the lobby at street level. She could buzz in any visitors, but she wasn't expecting anyone.

She walked over to the speaker, pressed the button, and said, "Yes?"

"Delivery for apartment 5C is what it says on my package."

Jill was on alert and replied, "I'm sorry. I didn't order anything so I won't accept that delivery."

Jill heard noise in the background and realized that another resident was entering the building and thought to do a favor for the delivery person.

She pressed the speaker button and yelled, "Don't let him in the building!" But it was too late.

"Madison, we have someone on the way here with a package of some sort. I don't know what it is, but we're not expecting anything, and we should treat it as a weapon. Speaking of weapons, time to grab something to defend ourselves. I'll take this lamp base, and why don't you get some vinegar out of the kitchen and put it in that spray bottle?"

They rushed to get items in their hands, and before they were ready, heard a knock on the apartment door as someone called out, "Delivery."

Jill yelled through the door, "Like I told you downstairs, I'm not expecting anything so you can return the package to whoever sent you here."

Her cell phone vibrated with a text just then.

I have a delivery person on their way to provide the written copy of our investigation so far into this case.

"Whoops, Madison. It seems like this package might be from James Davis."

"I think I'll still stand behind you with my spray bottle. Better to be safe than sorry."

Jill nodded and opened the apartment door to see the delivery man walking toward the end of the hallway with an envelope in his hands.

"Sir, sorry for the trouble I caused you. I understand that package really is for me," Jill said, holding out her hand.

The man turned around in the hallway and returned to the apartment door. He handed her the package and left. Jill went back inside and put the package on the kitchen counter and went to search for a knife to open it. She felt her phone vibrate again and pulled it out before opening the package.

The delivery person is approaching your street. Can you meet them out front?

Jill looked over at the package and said to Madison, "Grab my laptop and your purse. We need to exit this apartment, now!"

Madison saw the alarm in Jill's face and followed her to the door. In the hallway she said, "That's a fake delivery package. I don't know what's in it, but I'll let someone else open it who's wearing protective gear. I'll have to wash my hands outside."

Jill dialed Davis and he answered after a few rings. "Davis."

"Madison and I are walking to the front of the apartment building to meet your delivery person."

"Good."

"No, not good. I just received an envelope from a delivery person moments ago. We've left it unopened on the kitchen counter and are evacuating to the lobby. If indeed your delivery person shows up with a different envelope in a few moments, then you'll have to send a hazmat team to my apartment in order to open the envelope."

"Special Agent Ortiz warned me that you have a knack for attracting trouble. I guess she's not wrong. Stay on the phone with me so we can confirm the delivery from my person. She's an avid cyclist and goes everywhere in DC on a bicycle."

"I see a cyclist just turning the corner and slowing down coming toward my building. What's her name?"

"Lily Chong."

Jill went outside to the curb after looking up and down the street. She washed her hands as best she could in a cold outdoor faucet, then approached the cyclist after drying her hands on nearby plants.

"What's your name?" Jill asked the cyclist.

"Lily Chong and here's my ID badge." Jill took a quick look at the lanyard around the woman's neck and her picture and name matched.

She took the envelope and stepped back inside the building for safety's sake. Then she said into the phone, "James, can you send that hazmat team I mentioned? The envelope may be nothing, and then again it may be something. I'm going to find a new address."

She ended the call and then called Nathan.

"Think of something you want me to add to the grocery list?" he asked.

"No, we had a problem at our building again. I need to move us to new digs and your food will be unrefrigerated until I find a new location."

"I might have a location for us. Let me call you right back. Are you in a safe spot at the moment?"

"Yes."

"Good."

The call ended and Madison asked, "What's inside the envelope?"

"Maybe nothing, maybe a small explosive, maybe aerosolized talcum powder, maybe a threat of anthrax."

Her phone rang and it was Nathan. "I have new digs for us.

You can thank my contacts in the wine world. I'll finish my shopping here and head directly to the new address. I assume you'll pack up my stuff. Did you have another intruder?"

"No, maybe nothing, maybe something much worse. A fake courier delivered a package to the apartment minutes ahead of an official courier arriving. I handled it and it's sitting on the kitchen counter. It may contain nothing or it could be something bad. Hazmat is on its way."

"I texted you the new address. Do you need my help there?"

"No. It's about to become a three-ring circus and I don't like being a ringmaster. If you're safely tucked up in our new place, I won't have to worry about you."

"Hey, I married you for richer and poorer, in sickness and health, in trouble and safe, till death do us part."

Jill smiled at his words, "I don't remember that exact sentence in our wedding vows, but thanks for making me smile. Maybe your line was, 'I promise to make you laugh when someone is trying to harm you.'"

"Love you, Babe," he said before they ended the call.

Madison saw the smile and asked, "Okay, you have to share whatever Nathan said to make you smile. I could use a little humor right now."

"He tried to tell me that our wedding vows included the phrase 'in trouble and safe till death do us part.'"

"Oh, that's sweet," Madison said, relaxing a little.

"We have a new address thanks to his connections. I need to get back into the apartment to collect our stuff. He's going to be at the new location in about an hour. We may not be done here in an hour, but I'd like you to head over to the new location and work while I handle things here."

"Are you sure you can carry the possessions of all three of us?"

"Probably not, but I should have some helping hands here."

They looked down the street to see a van approaching with flashing lights, and it was red in color.

"This must be our hazmat people. Another new experience that you can add to your training hours or your résumé," Jill said.

The van identified itself as belonging to the District's fire department. When the driver got out of the vehicle, Jill walked over to him and introduced herself.

She recounted the issue with the envelope and its present location. She also indicated that she had handled the envelope with her bare hands and had since washed them at an outdoor faucet. She gave him the pass key to the building and her apartment.

He then briefed his crew on the situation. They gathered equipment and entered the building. Two of them had stayed behind, one to stay with the vehicle and the other to talk to Jill.

"Ma'am, I understand you were potentially exposed to an unknown substance. If you don't mind, I'd like to run a few tests on your hands."

"Go right ahead. By the way, I'm a forensic pathologist and I'm board-certified in toxicology, so feel free to talk technical to me."

"Yes, ma'am.

He swabbed her hands in a variety of places after understanding how she grasped the envelope. She was pleased to see that all the tests came back negative. Whether that was due to the fact that she had washed her hands, or the envelope never had anything toxic in it, would be unknown until they tested it.

A short while later the crew returned to the front of the building to speak with her.

"Ma'am, we found talcum powder on the envelope, and a pink glue smoke bomb inside," the leader said, pointing to one of his crew now covered with pink sparkles. "There was nothing toxic other than having pink sparkles stuck to his uniform."

"That's good news, and I guess your crew member is ready for a tea party with a group of little girls. Was there any note inside the envelope?"

"No ma'am. Here is the envelope if you would like to keep it."

"Maybe the FBI can fingerprint it," Jill said, noting that the hazmat crew were wearing gloves.

"Maybe."

Jill called Nathan and let him know that all was well and she and Madison would be packing up and moving soon. Within the hour, they were on their way to the new location.

"The neighbors in this building will be glad to see us leave. There have been three police visits and now a hazmat," Jill said.

"I know. I warned my father of all the activity, but told him there was no damage despite all of this activity.

They needed multiple loads to get everything to Melanie's car in the underground parking area. Once packed, Melanie was ready to drive to the new location which also had an underground parking area. Jill performed surveillance as they left and then watched their rear for anyone following them, but it was getting dark and that was hard. Still, she had Melanie stop at a shopping center parking structure before exiting and continuing to their new location, which was in Georgetown. By the time they reached the complex it was dark and Nathan met them at the gate arm for the parking structure. He followed the car in, making sure no one and no car followed behind them. Melanie would have given him a ride to their parking spot, but the car was full, so Nathan just followed behind.

She parked and Jill got out and gave him a hug before they began unloading the car. She could wait to settle into their space as she had lost time on the case, she was hungry, and she had received emails from Jo and Marie. The answer to the case conceivably was in those emails. When the emails had arrived, she sent them a brief text explaining that she was in the middle of a hazmat situation and would get to them later that evening. Both friends texted her back, *Are you okay?* to which she responded that she was good.

CHAPTER 17

adison and Jill explored their apartment, which wasn't as large as the last one, but was in a busier pedestrian area which offered some protection. The apartment had three bedrooms and a nice kitchen for Nathan. Jill found space in the living room to once again tape her murder board to the wall. A short time later she was ready to get to work. As Madison was still using her laptop, Jill pulled out her tablet to look at the emails. They were dense emails and so she asked Nathan to connect her tablet to the TV so she could read it on a large screen.

The three of them read first Marie's email and then Jo's.

"Wow, what made the members of the militia nominate these birdbrains to lead their group?" Jill asked.

Nathan replied, "Like many screwed up organizations, I suspect that these three men are narcissists and charismatic. Remember, you think you're dealing with a militia and organized crime, but you're dealing with a cult. People are following whatever their leader says to do."

"I think my secret power is the ability to see through people's haze of lies. I've never understood why cults work."

"There are a fair number of people in this world who lack direction. The militia gives them family and someone to give them orders. If they lack the knowledge of where to go next and what to do with their life, then the militia, gang, or cult fills in those pieces."

"You're right, but wow this stuff is unbelievable."

"People believe what they want to believe and often seek out friendship with only those who confirm their opinions. Most people do that whether they belong to a cult or not."

Jill sighed and spent some time studying the screen. The men at the top had salaries listed at over half a million each. Not bad for operating a nonprofit militia with fewer than one thousand members. The three men founded the militia and operated it without input from members. Jill bet the rank-and-file militia members were unaware of their leaders' salaries.

"I understand the militia leadership and how it works and who it attracts. What is the connection to the Cottonne Family?" Jill asked Nathan and Madison. "How does a militia benefit organized crime?"

"Hopefully this isn't a stereotype of what I see on TV, but could they be laundering money through the militia?" Madison asked.

"That's a good question. Let's look at what Jo has here," Jill went back and forth between the dues indicated on the report and the number of militia members.

"Madison, I think you're onto something. There is a lot more income reported than I believe actual militia members are paying. Looking at their reported income for dues would mean that each militia member is paying more than one thousand dollars for membership. This seems too much for what they get out of it. If you look at the expense side, they have a huge list of activities and I would bet that none of them are actually occurring. The members are likely not looking at these reports, so they don't know what they're missing. Many militias get together to practice their marksmanship skills and if they buy their own ammunition, and use someone's remote property, then who knows the difference? So maybe it really is just a front to launder money. The leaders just have to rehash some crazy ideas now and then and everyone sings Kumbaya."

"Okay, but then what about your missing plates? How does that fit into the picture?" Nathan asked.

Jill paused for a moment with an idea just on the edge of her brain. "So our earlier research showed that North Korea was one of the biggest counterfeiters of US dollars. Would an organized crime family sell plates to the North Koreans?"

"Gee whiz this is getting complicated," Madison said. "How did we start with a homicide and end up with militias, crime families, and the North Koreans?"

"North Korea runs counterfeit operations, but there have been major counterfeit operations run in North America. There's a Canadian who did well. Also, the UK tried to undermine the US in the Revolutionary War, and the North did so against the South in the Civil War. The US has actively accused North Korea of counterfeiting, but somehow I think it's a stretch to have this elaborate operation's end result be selling currency plates to North Korea," Jill said. "Let's look at our not-so-short list of suspects and see if anyone has printing experience among the security force staff. Beyond the executives, I would guess that a few of the rank-and-file militia members are plants to keep the leaders informed," Jill said.

"Have there been any other deaths among the militia men or the Bureau of Printing and Engraving staff?" Nathan asked.

Jill banged her hand against her head and said, "Duh, why didn't I think of that? Thank you, Sweetie."

"See, I'm good at something besides cooking."

"You have many skills besides cooking," she said, and gave him a hug before settling down and typing away.

Her first question was when was the militia founded, and that would be in their application for nonprofit status. Nonprofits had to report their financial activity every year to the IRS to keep that nonprofit standing. She pulled out a few of their forms and found that they were founded a decade ago and the three leaders had held their positions for the lifetime of the nonprofit. That begged the question as to whether other plates were stolen before this recent rash of thefts. She sent that question to Davis along with, "When the Bureau determines that a plate is no longer good, how do they dispose of it, and are any currency plates at the end of their lifecycle missing?" In theory, those plates were still somewhat useful or maybe someone with metal-plating expertise could renew them.

Then she paused a moment to think about how to find deaths among the two groups—the militia and the Bureau. Not every family placed a public funeral notice. Perhaps the best place to look was social media. She started down that path when her phone rang. It was Davis calling.

"You asked two interesting questions. We're researching the answers to them now. The Bureau leadership is finding the answers and will get back to me. Why did you ask those questions?"

"Actually, my husband suggested them. We were running down a rabbit hole on counterfeiters, and he threw the question on prior deaths at me. Then, as I read these stories about counterfeiters, I thought the used currency plates from the Bureau would likely have value so where did they end up?"

"The Bureau should have thought of that as well. The militia leaders have been in place since its founding a decade ago. It appears by looking at their IRS filings that they are laundering money. So maybe the local mafia set up the militia to launder money, but then decided to go after counterfeiting, maybe after a bunch of Bureau workers were talking about the currency lying around at their factory. I could see that inspiring these leaders to get their own chunk of cash. Maybe when the mafia created this militia, they targeted workers from the Bureau. I don't know, I'm just throwing out ideas."

"Those are some interesting theories. I'll get my people to help get you some answers. These so-called leaders of the militia—what else do they have on their résumés?"

Jill knew Marie had researched that somewhere, and she looked through her notes for the answer.

"I don't think they've had jobs other than working for the family business. That's the assessment from the HR expert on my team."

"Okay, you've given me some new data to have my team work up. I'll forward the other information to you as soon as I get it," Davis said, and they ended their call.

Madison announced she had access to the road cameras and so she went to work on identifying the motorcyclist who likely put the deadly ricin in Ed Thomas's delivered food.

Jill returned to social media looking for other Bureau deaths and she found three thanks to people's comments on social media. The other three were ruled heart attacks as well. Jill didn't have their medical history and so the cause of death might have been accurate. She forwarded that information to Davis and suggested he get a subpoena to pull the records from the medical examiner's office.

Jill felt that special zing when she was close to making a break-through on a case. She knew the answer wasn't going to be that North Korea was up to its usual shenanigans. Instead, it was going to be organized crime. North Korea wouldn't try to buy plates from the United States; rather, they would instead try to make their own. It was intriguing, but it didn't answer the question of the motorcyclist's identity who delivered the tainted food.

"Madison, how's the motorcycle search coming?"

"Actually, this software is fabulous. I wonder if I could buy a license from Henrik? I have at least ten views so far, but none of them has his helmet removed. I have got the license plate, but if they are at all smart, it will be a fake or a stolen plate or a stolen motorcycle."

"I have a feeling that Henrik won't sell this exact system to you, but maybe he'll have a different version for PIs."

"Why?"

"I think he would develop a bad reputation for violating everyone's privacy. I think he believes it only belongs in the hands of the military or law enforcement."

"Well, we're sort of law enforcement."

"True, but can you imagine how great this system would be for a domestic-violence abuser? They would have little trouble following their intended target."

"Oh, yes, I can see his concern."

"As far as I know, I'm the only person outside of law enforcement in the world to have a copy, and it's only because I solved his wife's murder and he knows he can trust me with the power of the system. I'm sure he doesn't want to get into the business of verifying every person's integrity who wants a copy of his software no matter the cost. He also jokes that I use his system so often around law enforcement people that he should make me a VP of sales. I seem to generate sales for him."

"Okay, I'll let the dream go as I get his point. That's cool that he recognizes your role in selling more copies."

While they were chatting they could hear pings, which meant the software was making matches to what they sought.

"We're up to forty matches now."

Jill nodded and her email alerted her that a new message arrived from Davis. She opened up her email and read:

There have been four deaths at the Bureau in the past five years. All of the deaths have been in the group that operates the currency-making machinery.

And a second forwarded message relayed more interesting data:

The currency plates are returned to the manufacturer to be melted down. They went back over their inventory and found that another six plates over the past five years haven't been returned to them. Both the Bureau and the company are revising their procedures. But . . ."

Jill sent back a request for Davis to check with someone in the Treasury Department about counterfeiting: Have they noticed an increase in counterfeit bills in the States or overseas? She didn't understand yet what was being done with the currency plates. She thought that the sale of the counterfeit dollars would earn more than the sale of the plates. The data that she reviewed in her earlier counterfeit research said that three dollars out of every one hundred thousand were determined to be fake. Surely someone in the Treasury Department had their thumb on changes in counterfeit currency.

Then, as always, Jill circled back to who killed Ed Thomas. Hopefully they would find the motorcyclist soon, but what was the motive for ending his life? Did he tell someone that he had currency plates with him? Or was it a bullying tactic of the militia whereby they said he must have sold currency plates to pay for his daughter's start-up, likely knowing full well that it wasn't true? Maybe the militia got word that he was undercover and it was revenge. Perhaps they were angered that he wouldn't join their militia that they saw as an extension of their military service. Okay, she needed to move on as there were many different motives, and identifying the motorcyclist would lead to the motive being revealed and she was wasting her time speculating.

She tuned back onto Madison's computer search and asked, "Any great pictures so far?"

There was silence and so Jill looked over to where Madison was staring at her laptop. She raised her eyes and said, "OMG, it's a woman. Her last name is Poli. Angelina Poli. I wonder if she's related to one of those three executives, or is Poli a common Italian surname?"

"Poison is the murder weapon of choice for females. Still, I'm surprised as this has been such a male-dominated investigation. Let me call Agent Davis and Detective Chambers."

Jill spoke to both men: "I'm not sure whose jurisdiction rodeo this is, so I'm notifying both of you that we have an identification for the motorcyclist who delivered Ed's poisoned food. What we don't have is her administering the poison on camera. She's related to one of the executives of the militia. Why don't you come over to our apartment and I'll run you through the footage?"

They agreed to be there within twenty minutes. Jill was starting to get hungry and said to Nathan, "What's for dinner?"

"Hunting for killers always raises your appetite. Do you want me to feed your guests?"

Jill thought for a moment and said, "I'm not sure. They may have already eaten. At the very least, Detective Chambers will be tracking down a judge to issue an arrest warrant. He may have to negotiate with Agent Davis as far as alerting the militia that they're being watched. Can you prepare something that would be easy to add a couple of extra plates if they want to join us?"

"Of course," Nathan said, and he went to work.

Jill worked on downloading footage so both men could leave with a recording identifying the motorcyclist as well the information from Henrik's system. Jill and Madison did as deep a search on Angelina Poli as they could before they heard the buzzer for their apartment.

Nathan verified Detective Chambers' identity and again when Agent Davis arrived about five minutes later. Once both men were seated to watch the video Jill prepared, Nathan called out, "Gentlemen, have you had dinner yet this evening? I can plate you some chicken breast and a new potatoes and vegetable medley, or we can eat the leftovers tomorrow."

They both looked surprised at the invite and nodded agreement, but then checked their watches. Jill watched the calculation in their brains and smiled. Who could resist a Nathan meal? He quickly plated the meals and everyone ate in the living room so they could watch the video of Angelina Poli. The two men ate like they were starved or a vacuum cleaned the plate. Before they started, Agent Davis said, "This is the first time I've had a consultant work overtime and come up with something very valuable on their first day of hire, and then feed me. Dr. Quint, you're setting an impossibly high bar that no one will ever match."

Jill laughed and said, "To be fair, my husband is feeding you. The food on your plate wouldn't have disappeared so fast if it had been me cooking."

Nathan smiled and asked, "Wine anyone? I know you're on duty, so I have coffee and tea as well."

"Tea," requested Chambers. "I'll likely be appearing before a judge in an hour or so and it wouldn't pay to have alcohol on my breath."

"I understand you're an expert artist in the wine industry and likely have the perfect pairing, so I'll have a glass of wine," said Agent Davis. Nathan handed Jill and Madison one as well.

The video was short and they watched it several times, but there was no recording of Angelina stirring anything into the food.

"This is enough to bring her in for questioning, but given her relationship with others in this complex situation, I'm sure she will lawyer up quickly," Detective Chambers said.

"Can you find out if this motorcycle belongs to her? Maybe we can catch her doing something else—like buying the castor beans," Jill asked.

"Just a moment," Chambers said, going through an app on his phone to look up the license plate. "Maybe we just got lucky. The motorcycle is registered to her. Where has she been the last couple of days?"

"Give Madison a few moments and we'll have a film put together for you. It would be even more helpful if you could get a GPS map of her cell phone. If she's identified on our system, the motorcycle is registered to her, and she visits Ed Thomas's apartment, that should be pretty convincing for a jury. Before you got here, we did some social media research work about Angelina. She's married to the treasurer, Thomas Poli. She's by his side for many militia functions according to the social network that they talk on. It's called Scat, and other militia groups discuss stuff that interests them."

"This is really good stuff," Davis said.

"Yes, but it's only half of the equation. We don't know a motive yet for the murder, and we don't know where the currency plates are located," Jill said. "By the way, we couldn't have done this without you giving us access to road cameras. Oh, and one more issue Ms. Poli lives in Virginia, so we can learn more about her if we can track her through Virginia and maybe Maryland also."

"I'll have access for you tomorrow morning. I would love to have you demo your system at Quantico. I know that the software's owner is a personal friend of yours and he was recently in the US from Germany, but I think having you demo this as an amateur is more powerful."As soon as he said "amateur." he put his hands up to stop Jill's eruption at the word. "In the eyes of the FBI, you're an amateur as you haven't been through any law-enforcement training."

"Actually, I had some training in order to get my PI license . . ."

"But my point is that you haven't been through any kind of extensive law-enforcement training academy, yet you operate this technology with ease. I see it as critical to our mission of finding missing and abducted children. We would find them quicker with that technology. So with you demonstrating its usefulness rather than a more sophisticated approach by the company's owner, we'll have people interested and on-board with using it sooner."

Jill sighed and said, "I hear what you're saying. In not so many words, you want me to shame the FBI into buying and using the technology as I can find answers sooner than your agency can if I use this tool."

"Yes, in not so many words."

"As you mentioned, the owner is a personal friend, so I'll ask his permission to do this. Someday the academy may want to send its agents to his home near Frankfurt. It would give your Hogan's Alley a run for your money. The Dutch and German police are using it. Back to the case at hand, Detective Chambers is going to go after Ms. Poli, and I'll meet your crew somewhere tomorrow—the Hoover Building or Quantico?"

"Hoover."

"Can you bring your BAU people to that meeting? I still don't feel like I understand the motive for Ed's death." Jill asked, and Davis nodded. "If we understood the motive, it might lead us to how the currency plates are being used."

Davis and Chambers left the apartment. Nathan was cleaning up in the kitchen and Jill needed to call Henrik. She glanced at the time and decided she would text him as it was the middle of the night in Germany, but she had no idea where he was. Then she looked over to Madison and said, "This is such a wacky case; you're going to be spoiled when asked to do some kind of cheating-person surveillance. Remember, when you feel that way, that you learn something from every case, every client, and the client is paying you for your work, no matter how tedious it is."

Before Madison could do more than nod, Jill's phone rang and it was Henrik.

"Hi Henrik. I got an offer from the FBI today and I wanted to run it by you as they want me to present your software rather than you."

"You're prettier than I am," he said, with European charm oozing across the phone call.

"Actually, they told me that they like that I'm an amateur."

"Oh my. Are they still living?"

"I sort of understand why women resort to using poison. Basically, 'if a dumb blonde like me can find usefulness in the system, then think what an experienced FBI agent could do with it' was the gist of the remark."

"You're sure you left them breathing?"

"You're good for my ego, Henrik. I was outraged when he made the statement, but he explained that I lack street cred because I didn't go to some law-enforcement academy. Despite my lack of education, I can still find criminals with the help of your system. Do you mind my demonstrating the system, knowing that it might be a purchasing presentation?"

"You don't give yourself credit. We've talked in the past about you being my VP of marketing and you turned me down. I feel completely comfortable with you demonstrating my system."

"Thanks, Henrik. I appreciate your vote of confidence."

"You don't know all the bells and whistles of my software, but what you do know is how to find criminals with it, and that's all your audience is looking for, so keep that in mind."

Jill had moved into her bedroom when she took the call as she wanted to ask Henrik a question in private.

"Henrik, Madison, my intern, said she wanted to buy a copy of the system to help her with investigations. I sort of thought you had a policy of only selling to law-enforcement agencies because there's powerful information and you don't know who is a legitimate PI and who is a domestic-violence stalker. Did I get that right?"

"You did. You are the sole person outside of my company with a personal copy of the software and for exactly the reason you mention. Law-enforcement agencies have bad apples in them, but when I implement my software for a police force, I set up reports so that they know if someone's using the system to do background searches on people rather than to collar criminals."

They talked a little about her case, and Henrik had heard some of the information from Marie, whom he was dating.

"Counterfeiting currency is one of the oldest criminal activities in the modern world. It's the 21st century, and we're still chasing counterfeiters. Good luck with that."

"Thanks, Henrik. By the way, I invited the FBI to your home to try out your obstacle course without asking you. Oops."

Henrik was chuckling as they ended the call.

Jill returned to the living room and said, "Sorry, I needed to take that call as I never know where in the world Henrik is calling from. I did verify that he only sells his software to law-enforcement groups as he requires as part of the installation that reports of activity be generated so it is obvious when people are searching for private information that is not case related. With individuals there's the potential for abuse. You shouldn't need his information on the majority of your cases as the perp will be obvious, but you can always call me and I may be able to help."

Madison nodded and she really couldn't argue with the reasoning. Jill was lucky, but then, she had solved the deeply personal case of his wife's murder. Furthermore, from what she understood, Nathan worked with Henrik with a vineyard he owned. Oh well, Jill was right that it would be years before she assisted in complicated cases like this one.

"We've been at this all day and evening. Let's let the software run overnight and then we'll take a rideshare service to the Hoover Building. Remind me to remind the detective to inform Melanie Thomas that we're making progress on identifying her father's killer."

"This has been a long and strange day. I'll program the software to track Angelina's motorcycle for the previous two weeks before the murder."

CHAPTER 19

The next morning, Jill and Madison were escorted to a conference room in the Hoover Building. Once again, they made temporary nameplates, as did everyone who came into the conference room. Jill silently laughed at all those acronyms on the nameplate. They had to know she was a civilian and had no idea what any of the initials meant.

James Davis chaired the meeting and started with an update on what they had discovered since they left the conference room the day before. Detective Chambers was not in the room, but Davis has spoken with the detective and provided a summary of the conclusions about Angelina Poli and what little she said during her interview.

"The inventor of a software system that is being used in some law-enforcement agencies across the US and Europe is a personal friend of Dr. Quint. I observed her and her assistant use the system to track our suspect's motorcycle as she delivered poisoned food to our Bureau of Printing and Engraving under-cover agent to his apartment. While she's going to demonstrate how it was used to search for a motorcycle, I want everyone in the room to think about how it might be used to find missing and abducted children. Dr. Quint, the room is yours."

She hooked up her computer to the projector and went over the new information. The overnight search showed the computer had found numerous locations, including an organic food store that might have sold castor beans which were the source of the poison that killed Ed Thomas, and she sent that piece of information over to the detective, as he was leading the case against Angelina Poli. She also did a search of Ms. Poli's address and found castor bean plants around her front landscaping.

"I'm also a Board Certified Toxicologist and have a bachelor's degree in botany. Those plants could have their beans harvested to make ricin. At this time of year, there are no beans on the plants, but you can collect and store them for months or even years."

Once she finished her demonstration and answered all questions, she asked the room at large for a motive for the murder of Ed Thomas. The consensus from the behavioral psychologists was that the executives of the militia fed their members with false information. They did a thorough job of smearing Ed's reputation to the workforce. Half of his co-workers believed he had stolen the currency plates on behalf of the militia, but then kept them for himself so he could fund his daughter's start-up company. The other half of the employees believed he was a thief and stole the plates from the Bureau and sold them on the open market for cash. It was a squishy motive, but one that she'd thought of herself as well.

"Yes, but was that enough for murder?"

"Someone must have informed the leaders that Thomas was working undercover for us. That's the motive that makes the strongest sense to me. I think this militia must have members in a few key areas to gather information," Davis offered, and Jill agreed.

She concluded that she had done everything she could to

solve the Ed Thomas murder. Now, it was time to turn her attention to the missing currency plates. First, she obtained a currency plate picture from the internet and had her software search for it around the date that the leader said it went missing. She got no hits. Next she tried flat four-by-four boxes leaving the Bureau around the time of the theft. She got a significant number of hits for that and began to review each picture as she worked. She deleted each irrelevant picture. She was perhaps halfway through when a photo came up of a man carrying a large flat box a day before the currency plate was reported missing. Jill used the software's facial-identity feature to locate his name.

"His name is William Wilson, and he's an employee of the security force. The box he is carrying would fit a currency plate, but we have no indication of what's inside." She went through more pictures and found another security staff member carrying the same type of box as Wilson.

"What would you do next with this information?" someone asked. "By the way, I'm convinced we need this software system. Does anyone else agree with me?" There were many nods of agreement and verbal "yeas" around the room.

"I would talk to your warehouse people and find out what kind of supplies arrive in such a box. Perhaps William took it home because he's moving to a new apartment and didn't want his pictures on the wall damaged in the move. However, if your inventory folks say that they don't take delivery of such a box, it becomes much more suspicious, and I would question William and the second man whom I have now identified as John Wong. I think it's unusual that both men would be leaving with such a box, and they each are carrying the box like there is some weight inside of them."

"Are these two members of the militia?"

"We don't have an exact list as that is not required anywhere in the official filings of the group. My assistant and I did find many members of a social network that caters to militia groups, but that's not an accurate way to identify who is a member."

While Jill was talking and demonstrating the technology, Madison was doing a background search on Wilson and Wong.

"I have some information on Wilson and Wong. In searching for their names on social media and in the militia discussion group, it would appear that they both are a part of the militia. We have no proof that they paid dues, but they talk about their brothers-in-arms in reference to the militia group."

"Any mention of the plates?

"Something better, I think. I have a picture of the cardboard box being opened and the currency plate pulled out. Gosh, these guys are dumb," Madison said, and several people rushed from their seats to see what Madison had on her screen.

"Make sure you save it as it is evidence." Madison took a picture with her phone, then saved the image.

Jill brought the projector cord over and soon everyone in the room was looking at the large picture of the currency plate being pulled out of the box. Jill noticed other faces in the picture and put the images through the facial-recognition system and soon had the group identified. She passed the information along to the agents. There was action happening around the room and Jill and Madison were all but forgotten.

Jill leaned in and whispered, "Great job at research. We just beat them in a head-to-head competition. Pretty sweet, huh?" Jill held her hand up for a fist bump, and Madison likewise held her hand up.

"Let's pack up and head back to the apartment. I want to speak to Detective Chambers and see what happened during the interview with Angelina Poli. Law enforcement has work to do to bring people in for questioning and search for the plates and any currency they may have produced. I'll just let Agent Davis know that we are heading home but that we'll be searching for additional information."

"I wonder if they have a gadget or detector for counterfeit currency? I know that some retail locations mark higher denomination currency with a pen and hold it up to light and it may be as simple as that," Madison asked.

"There's a reason for your question. Why do you want a detector?" Jill replied.

"I was thinking they should test any currency that Angelina Poli or any of our stupid criminals in the picture have in their possession. Wouldn't that be forensic evidence?"

"It would and that's a good idea. We'll talk to Detective Chambers and find out what's going on with Ms. Poli," Jill said, making note of Madison's comment.

They left the Hoover Building intent on walking toward the Capital Mall to catch the metro home. They could have taken a ride-share service, but it was a nice walk across a very important part of the District as it contained so many monuments. It was an area heavy in pedestrians—both government workers and tourists. Jill considered whether someone might follow them, but then they would have had to know that she had had a meeting in the Hoover Building. Jill looked around her, but there were simply too many people about to guess if they were being followed. Still, it was a lesson she should tell Madison about.

"We could be followed at the moment, but there are simply too many people going about their business for us to guess. Still, when we get down to the metro tracks, let's stay in the center of the platform until the train arrives. I wouldn't want anyone to push us onto the tracks."

"Geez, I'm walking down the street enjoying the glow of finding information for the FBI and I forget all about the criminals who could be all around us here."

"Don't worry about it. I just concluded that there were too many people for me to tell if we were being followed. This is a very busy area, between tourists and government types. Let's just not stand near the tracks. In fact, you're harder to push from a seated position, so no matter how dirty the seat, we'll sit down until our train is in front of us on the tracks."

Jill saw a nice place to sit up ahead and said, "Let me call the detective before we go underground, as we may not have a signal."

Madison nodded and they sat. Madison kept watch while Jill dialed the detective.

"Dr. Quint. I was about to call you. How did the meeting go at the Hoover Building?"

"Some of these militia guys will make the dumb criminals list in the future. Madison found a picture of someone opening a box that we had noted the employee exiting with. The photo captured the currency plate."

"I love criminals who make my day so easy," he chuckled. "Likewise Ms. Poli set herself up for failure. She admitted to owning and riding the motorcycle. We got a search warrant for the house and found castor beans and counterfeit money inside. That's sheer arrogance that we would never catch up with her is amazing."

"Did she indict her husband and the other executives?"

"She did, given the evidence lying around. We have a warrant out for his arrest at the moment."

"Oh? I thought she would have lawyered up and her husband would immediately come to her aid."

"Actually, I think he set her up to take the fall based on what she said during her interview and the evidence he left around the house. I think he must have known that she was going to be too slow of a thinker to get herself out of trouble. She'll be fun to watch when she goes on trial, but at the moment we are holding her without bail."

"So you have a warrant out for Mr. Poli's arrest?" Jill asked.

"We do, as well as the other two executives. Once she realized her husband wasn't coming to her aid, she gave us dirt on the other two also. We have identified our letter writer per Ms. Poli. She said it was the VP—Michael Messina. I think you were one of the people who believed that the executives started rumors to make the militia behave in certain ways, including shunning Ed Thomas. However, the leaders couldn't make anyone in the militia mad enough to kill Ed, so she took care of it as the 'Boss's woman.' Those are her words, not mine."

"Wow, that's some screwed-up thinking. Michael Messina was not on our radar as the letter writer. I don't believe he served in the military with Ed Thomas."

"According to Ms. Poli, Messina interviewed one of the militia members who did serve with Ed. The point of the letters was to scare Mr. Thomas."

"That was a dumb criminal move as Melanie Thomas would have never hired me if she hadn't been aware of the threatening letters. His death would still be considered a homicide, but it would have been investigated by your staff and then eventually, the FBI," Jill said.

"Yes. Every day I seem to be disappointed by one of our fellow humans."

"So, what's everyone's thinking about these three militia executives on the run? Have they left the country? Is the mafia family protecting them? Do they have a nice pile of counterfeit money to travel around the world with?"

"We don't know. Those are questions best answered by your FBI friends."

"Maybe I'll see if Agent Davis can continue our access to the road cameras in this area and my software can track them to their new hiding place."

"That would be helpful. I'll call him as his group is involved in this mess and we'll see if we can use your skills to locate the men," Detective Chambers said.

Shortly thereafter, they ended the call, and Jill and Madison continued their route to the metro system. They had a few stops before their exit closest to Georgetown. Jill didn't quite know where the Georgetown perimeter was exactly located, but last night she'd taken a moment to look up the metro system, and the exit she selected would get them within five blocks of their apartment.

Jill surveyed everyone in the car with them and she thought that a man at the other end of the car was suspicious. He sort of looked like one of their three suspects. Jill doubted her vision and asked Madison to verify. The girl faked like she was using her phone app to apply lipstick, all the while she was snapping pictures. The man had a bag which could be filled with clothes to leave town with, counterfeit money, or maybe even weapons. The women agreed he was suspicious.

"Is this second man with him?" Madison asked, pointing to one of her pictures. Jill nodded.

"Let's stay in this car until we see a large surge of people standing up to exit."

That turned out to be the stop that was closest to the apartment. Jill had texted Nathan as well as the detective, when she saw the first sign of trouble. She hoped that the texts would reach them from the underground. She let them know where they were getting off the route. That meant that Nathan would have time to jog the few blocks to the subway stop. She hoped the detective would also get officers to this stop if the man followed them off at the stop. In the crush of people exiting and hurrying up the stairs and escalator to leave the station, it was hard to see where their suspect was. Madison was at work with her phone using the selfie function to see what was going on behind them while Jill was studying who was in front of them. She was relieved to see Nathan's head pop up near the top of the escalator.

"I see a couple of men pushing their way slowly toward us. It's going to be close as to whether we get off this escalator or if they reach us first."

Jill looked again at the top and relaxed a little when she saw two uniformed officers take up position on either side of Nathan.

"Have they guys slowed their ascent to us?"

"Yes, how did you know? Now they're turning and making their way back down. They're not making any friends on this escalator."

About the time they reached the top, Detective Chambers had joined the welcoming party.

"Where are they?"

"They're nearly at the bottom of the escalator," Madison described the men who the officers could see were pushing people out of the way to get down into the station and escape on a subway car. The officers took off down the down escalator. Jill was sure they would get caught eventually; the subway cameras would track their movements.

"How did they know to follow us?" Madison asked.

"I'm guessing they knew Melanie Thomas hired us or my picture was taken that day we raided the Bureau."

"Okay, but how did they know where to follow us?"

"Good question. Perhaps one of the guys who were arrested for breaking into our old apartment dropped a tracking device into a purse or backpack before we conked them on the head. Maybe they've had surveillance on us from the time we arrived here. I don't know how they found us, and I didn't bring my tracking-device detector with me."

"I'll have someone come over and scan your stuff as you won't have peace from these men until we have them locked away," said the detective.

Jill nodded and then paused for a moment to think.

"I think we have fulfilled our duties to Melanie Thomas and to the FBI with the identification of who has the currency plates. I think we can all leave in the morning, right, Detective?"

"Dr. Quint, you've done a great job solving the murder of Ed Thomas. I can't speak for my Fed friends, but you probably should call Agent Davis about this latest activity. I might be able to assign guards to your apartment today, and you can head home early in the morning."

"That sounds like an excellent plan!" Nathan said. "It's time to go home to our fur babies and the quiet life of growing grapes."

Jill snorted over his last few words. Both Detective Chambers and Madison wondered about the story behind that snort, but were too polite to ask at that moment. Instead, they all shook hands and departed on the busy street walking back to the apartment. The men by now likely had caught a subway car to somewhere else, but for now, Jill, Nathan, and Madison were safe and ready to take on a new case.

The End

ABOUT THE AUTHOR

I reside in Northern California with my rescue dog and cat. I love to travel, play sports, read, and drink wine and beer. I enjoy the diversity of the world and I'm always watching people and events for story ideas. All of my stories are generated by my imagination, I don't use AI to write books.

If you would like to sign up for my bi-weekly blog and announcement of new books, please follow this link: https://www.AlecPecheBooks.com

While you're waiting for the next story, if you would be so kind as to leave a review for this book, that would be great. I appreciate all the feedback and support. Reviews buoy my spirits and stoke the fires of creativity.

Readers that sign up for my blog receive a free prequel novelette for the Jill Quint Series.

Now You Don't See Me

Where Did She Go?

How Did She Get There?

<u>Dog Humor</u>

Eat, Play, Poop: Letters to my parents from camp

<u>New Urban Fantasy Series - Stephanie Jones</u>

The Awakening at Lake Tahoe (short story)

Witch's Medicine (2024)